REALITY WORKS

Let It Happen

Chandra Alexander

Red Wheel
Boston, MA / York Beach, ME

First published in 2002 by
Red Wheel/Weiser, LLC
368 Congress St.
Boston, MA 02210
www.redwheelweiser.com

Cataloging-in-Publication Data available on request from the Library of Congress.

ISBN 1-59003-009-5
Typeset in Perpetua
MV

Printed in the United States of America

08 07 06 05 04 03 02
8 7 6 5 4 3 2 1
The paper used in this publication meets the minimum requirements of the
American National Standard for Information Sciences—Permanence of Paper
for Printed Library Materials Z39.48-1992 (R1997).

For the spirit of "Rosie" everywhere . . .
December 26, 1980–Infinity

CONTENTS

ACKNOWLEDGMENTS

I would like to acknowledge and thank those who, in this world of constant change, remain steadfast, never wavering, always loving:

- Paul Dragon, for believing in the abundance of the universe and proving it by spoiling me rotten.

- Gary Goodman, for driving me back to my roots and allowing me to finally say good-bye.

- Andie Weiner, for seeing things I sometimes miss and encouraging my vulnerabilities.

- Daniel Watts, another four, for willingly sharing the self-conscious weird stuff as well as the "specialness."

- Michael Eggleston—my male side separated at birth—for "getting it" before I speak.

- Suki Murphy-Thomas, for late-night gossip and laughter (always delightful) and for her absolutely impeccable character.

- My brother Jed Alexander, for his sweetness and loving me unequivocally.

- Eddie Oliver, for always staying present and matching my "reality," regardless how strange.

- Leela Samartino, my soul sister, for giving unconditionally (it is her nature). She is more loyal than the sun.

- Baba, for the gift of discipline and a quiet mind. I will be eternally grateful.

- And to Jan Johnson, my publisher, who heard my voice and loved the book, I thank you.

INTRODUCTION

When something is real, it is as clear and raw as it gets. It is bottom-line, unequivocal, and not up for debate. It has both punch and promise. It often comes at the end of a long inner struggle, sometimes in the shower, sometimes driving in stop-and-go traffic, and always when we have consciously stopped thinking about it. What is real delivers peace.

But if we think of peace as a state of euphoria, we will be missing the key to what is probably the most misunderstood concept in spirituality. Peace is the result of clarity, a rock solid feeling that is stark and without embellishment of any kind. It is a place where, if only for the moment, there are no more questions. It has nothing to do with pleasure or pain. As a matter of fact, sometimes in the midst of horrific pain, with defenses dismantled and raw, we may suddenly "get it."

But touching our vulnerability frightens us so we quickly retreat to a well-known safe place, rationalizing whatever doesn't fit into our preprogrammed, hard-wired agenda. A button has been pushed and before we know it, we are riding a wave of momentum, a chain reaction of our stuff that closes our expanded heart. To support this delusion, we seek consensus for our opinion, asking others for their opinions until we get the answers we want. But just because two people have the same opinion of reality doesn't make it so, and we are once again left feeling confused and disconnected.

We will continue this way, perhaps for our whole life, until we consciously surrender thinking—our need to understand every-thing with the mind—and willingly open to *feeling*. In order to get even a glimpse of what is real and true, to "see" reality, we must be able to intimately touch our humanness, without rationalization or apology. We cannot indefinitely sanitize and sugarcoat this process simply because it scares us.

We may be able to fool ourselves for a while, but not forever. Regardless of how clever we are, reality is. There is no way around it. We can dress it up to appear more palpable, but it is, always and forever, human. It is only through our humanness that we can know our divinity, not the other way around. Only through the gutsy, messy stuff can we touch our essence. The dark places we run from—those are the places we need to go. What we are most afraid of sets us free.

As we endlessly discuss this bittersweet nature and publicly cel-ebrate the dual yet equal qualities of the yin/yang, joy, beauty, and success always win out, leaving as distant stepchildren sorrow, ugli-ness, and failure. We have been so conditioned to want only what is easy and initially makes us feel good that we have neglected the soft underbelly, that part of life that is difficult and makes us uncomfortable, but in the end has the ability to connect us to our core and make us whole.

It takes tremendous ego strength and internal fortitude to delve into unknown territory, hidden places with secrets we have so long avoided. In order to do this, we need to have a sense of Self that is strong enough to withstand scrutiny, criticism, and, finally, change. What is unknown is outside our conscious mind. It produces chaos, a feeling of being out of control. The more we are able to relinquish control and move out of our comfort zone, the more we are able to shift our distorted view to something that makes sense. If we are willing to sit with no safety net, squarely in the midst of our demons, what ostensibly appeared to be chaos becomes the energy that moves us out of that stuck place and provides us with the opportunity to grow. What initially is uncomfortable ultimately nourishes our soul.

When we are brave, the face of spirit reveals itself. It is a naked face, and its pristine beauty glows with the light of the Inner Self. It demands our recognition and offers us joy. If we are willing to stay in the moment and all that it offers, something unique happens. In a flash, we are catapulted into a new state of consciousness, a fresh way of seeing. Rather than feeling betrayed by this ever-changing universe, we delight in it and in wherever it might lead us. When we trust our feelings, we watch reality work and let it happen.

The essence of spirituality is this process—a human adventure that has the power to transform each and every one of us. When T. S. Eliot said, "It is ending up where you began but knowing the place for the first time," he took a very complicated concept and reduced it to something simple, yet elegant. His stripped-to-the-bone statement has the ability to transform us in an instant if we let it.

But to feel the power of his words, we must hear the words and not think about them. The minute we think, we lose the gestalt. What is real has nothing to do with thinking. It is intuitive, trusting, ever-changing. We must be willing to suspend the inner critic who is constantly trying to be in control, and just let go. It is only when we lose our self-consciousness, our need to make things happen, that things finally do begin to happen in a way that has both ease and grace.

What follows is my way of looking at the world. Although it is in my voice, it is my hope that the voice is real and deep enough to touch each of you in a place that resonates true for you. The various forms of experience may appear accidental, but they are never random and metaphorically always hold the key to deeper understanding of one's Self and how the universe unfolds. No one can tell us what something means. Only we know what it means for us.

Our moment of truth is exhilarating. Positioned solidly in the present, we are not confused. We are absolutely clear because we are congruent—our opinion of reality and how it really works are the same. With quiet mind, we let it happen; knowing the rhythm of the universe is in perfect harmony with our open heart.

This is what makes our life work.

If You're Bored With Your Story, It's Time To Change

There is nothing worse than hearing the same old story over and over again, and yet most of us have no trouble repeating *our* story. For some reason, we think our tale of woe is different and proceed to share the intimate details with all who will listen. We are oblivious to the blank stares and veiled yawns, and talk long after all interest has waned.

Friends and family mistakenly think they are providing a valuable service when they sit hour after hour feigning interest in what we have to say. They think this is what they are supposed to do, even though they have long since tired of hearing the same litany. They give us similar suggestions over and over again and in the process commiserate with our plight. The pattern is set for talks that go nowhere into the night.

So we keep on talking because no one tells us to be quiet.

Reality Works

One day, telling our story, we actually hear the words. What once had drama and seriousness now sounds narcissistic and funny. A crucial shift has taken place—we have gone from being victims to assuming responsibility for whatever happens in our lives. This change has allowed us to truly hear our words for the first time.

Listening, we hear repetitive themes and familiar complaints. Initially, we thought it was okay because the names, places, and faces were different. But if we are honest with ourselves, we know the truth—it is really the same old story. Nothing has changed.

Finally, we are bored.

So bored, we don't even bother to create a new story. We realize that they are all basically the same—none any better or worse than the other—just that mine is mine and yours is yours.

The simplicity of our realization is astounding. Not realizing that we were carrying around tons of garbage, we suddenly feel lighter. We take a moment to remember all the friends who sat through countless hours listening to this stuff, and we smile.

Would we do it for someone else? I don't think so.

Having let go of the drama, we embrace the adventure.

THE SPACE BETWEEN
THE OLD WAY NOT WORKING
AND THE NEW WAY NOT YET FOUND
IS WHERE CONSCIOUSNESS EXPANDS—
STAY IN THE GAP!

The Buddha sat under the Bodhi tree for forty years and asked him-self the quintessential question, "Who am I?" His patience was infi-nite and his resolve unyielding. He knew his old way of looking at the world had brought him pain and suffering; he also knew that there must be another way. As he asked himself the all-important question about essence, and heard the answers, he rejected them by saying, "Not this, not this, not this."

I imagine those forty years were fairly treacherous. From the time he sat down to the time he got up forty years later, a lot must have happened. I'm sure there were times that he just wanted to get up and leave. But he somehow knew the truth would take him to another place, and he was willing to go through it all to get there. Imagine the power that was at work. He had no idea where he was going. All he knew was that where he had been was not the answer. Through confusion, fear, anxiety, and darkness, he sat. Never knowing if there would be an end to his quest, he resolved to stay in the gap.

The gap between the old way no longer working and the new way not yet found is the only place that consciousness expands. To stay in that space takes tremendous courage and discipline. As familiar forms shift and mutate, what once was capable of making us feel secure and comfortable becomes a distant memory. It simply doesn't bring us happiness anymore. The energy is changing. We make a conscious choice to go with the energy rather than cling to the form. Something inside us is letting us know that if we want something more, we have to be something more. It is only when we move from the known to the unknown that energy has a place to stretch and expand and create new ways for us to express ourselves.

The space in between is always uncomfortable. The old forms have dropped away and have not been replaced. There is nothing to hang on to other than the romanticized remembrance of an exotic adventure. Like the Buddha, when we say, "Not this, not this, not this . . ." we are making an implicit commitment to accept only the truth and nothing else. When we tell the universe that we are not willing to do it the old way anymore, what we are actually doing is withdrawing our energy from that way.

As we withdraw the energy, we can instantly see the forms change. The relationship we thought we would die without suddenly loses its allure, and the job we were so scared to quit is something we no longer want. As we surrender to that place, a movement of new energy is at work. Although nothing has yet come to fruition, that doesn't mean things aren't changing. The darkness we are experiencing is a necessary prelude to a whole new way of doing things, and we stay in the gap until another door opens.

You Are Only Allowed To Think When You Can Feel

Can we ever really know anything with our intellect? We can analyze, dissect, and reassemble thoughts to create an acceptable reason that something is the way it is, but in order to touch the essence of something, we must be willing to bypass the mind and rest in the heart.

What we are talking about here is not the romantic or emotional heart, but that spot in the chest that resonates the truth. This is the home of the inner voice, the intuitive place that stretches far beyond the intellect into the caves of mystery and longing. To get there, we must pull the energy from above the neck to below it. This movement takes concerted effort, but it is worth it. As our point of concentration shifts and we become more comfortable with feeling rather than thinking, we enter the rarified zone of knowing.

Most people pride themselves on their ability to think and value a high I.Q. as though it were capable of delivering peace and contentment. But intellectual capacity is just that—it will never permit us to see to the core of things. It will always stop just short of the big banana—it simply doesn't have the power to pierce the illusion.

This is because it's not supposed to. The function of the mind is to operate in the world of dualities, and the intellect willingly obliges. Like the *Tao* says, when we find one thing beautiful, we automatically find another ugly. Only by dismissing one idea as worthless, does the intellect accept another as ideal.

But to really know something, we have to experience it unconditionally. And for that to happen, we have to step outside the mind. This process is not just devoid of thinking, it is beyond thinking. Even if all our thoughts line up and make perfect sense, that is not truth's final resting place.

To test the "realness" of something, we must feel it. When we feel, we end up in the body, not the mind. As the energy descends, it wells in the chest and expands. Suddenly we are aware of our body. This physical realization snaps us back and instantly makes us present. We are no longer one step away from the action, we are the action. Rather than thinking about our life, we are living it.

It is only from this place of feeling that our thinking has any real power. When we ask ourselves how we really feel and the answers are strong and clear, we know we are on the right path. Armed with this solid knowing, we are not looking for the mind to make us comfortable. We already know who we are and what will work for us.

In a spirit of confidence and playfulness, we offer this feeling of certainty to the mind. We are curious to see the various forms it will take and delight in the way the universe manifests our desires. Staying centered in the body, we allow the mind to freely develop the appropriate arenas. After all, this is what the mind does best.

Going from one form to another, it tests possible matches. And when the fit is right, we know it.

At last, all the pieces fit. No longer are we trying to whip the mind into submission or demand that it give us clarity. Our experience of clarity comes from the heart. The sequence is finally correct—first we feel, and then we think. This is the natural order of things.

It Is Our Fear
That Creates Our Bravery

We tend to think of bravery as something one-dimensional—either someone is brave or they are not. But we cannot simply decide to be brave. Real bravery results naturally from a state of being that is characterized by both fear and vulnerability.

So often we equate bravery with fearlessness, utter abandon in the face of danger. But can we really be brave when there is no fear and nothing worth protecting?

To understand bravery, we must first understand the nature of fear and also how true vulnerability occurs. Fear is neither good nor bad. It is simply a barometer that tells us we are entering unknown territory, uncharted waters. It signals the movement from a place known to a place unknown, and therein lies our fear.

To feel afraid and do it anyway is the movement toward real vulnerability. When we are willing to touch that soft underbelly, we open ourselves up to the possibility of great love as well as intense pain. Instinctively, we know that something so open contains it all, and we acutely feel the loss of control.

The soft underbelly is the true essence of spirituality, the part that has remained hidden. It keeps us trapped inside our walls, unable to touch one another. When we choose to expose it, we are making a statement to the universe that says, "I am tired of being separate. I am willing to risk leaving the safety of my shell for the possibility of truly feeling connected to another human being."

Armed with our fear in one hand and our vulnerability in the other, we move out into the world. Tentative at first, we gradually accept the seemingly conflicting feelings of staying and running. Something in us knows that it is this exquisite balance that creates an awareness that keeps us on the razor's edge. It is from this place and this place only that the warrior is created. He protects the soft underbelly, and the soft underbelly makes him brave. His courage is genuine. At long last he has a treasure worth protecting. He instantly springs full-blown prepared to defend the openness of his bounty. His fierceness is formidable. He is there to guard the wide-open spaces and guarantee that they stay open. He has fought long and hard, and each interior battle has taken him closer to home. He is not about to miss his calling.

TRUSTING THE BULLSHIT METER
ALWAYS GIVES US THE EDGE

Some call it a gut feeling, others intuition. Not matter what you call it, each of us has a little voice inside our heads. Sometimes the voice is loud, sometimes soft. Whether or not we listen to that voice—that is what makes all the difference.

We go through this world with our five senses. We are conditioned to dismiss anything we cannot see, smell, touch, taste, or hear and rely on our brain to translate the information we get into a form that makes sense. Restricting our world in this way gives us a sense of control but severely limits the way we receive messages.

The five senses are readily accepted by the intellect. We understand hearing because we can touch our ears and tasting because we have a mouth. But how do we explain the silent voice that says, "Turn here, not there" when we appear to have asked it nothing? Do we listen or do we disregard anything we can not explain?

How we answer this question intrinsically defines the quality of our life. Operating with just five senses, we are more or less on equal footing with all the other human beings out there. But by trusting a sixth sense—our intuition—we have the edge. When we listen to the voice that can't be explained, we give that voice power. The more we listen, the more it speaks to us.

An accurate bullshit meter is the most powerful tool we can have. There is nothing more potent than sixth sense information. It whispers what to offer in the final negotiation and instinctively moves us away from people who do not have our best interests at heart. It is a result of trust, believing that all the information we will ever need is available to us at any instant.

Some of us may be more intuitive than others, but that does not mean that this information is not available to us all. Like an atrophied muscle, unused intuition needs to be worked out. Slowly, softly the voice begins to speak. Sometimes we can barely hear what it is saying, sometimes it is nothing more than a nagging feeling to stop. Do we reject this feeling as frivolous or do we honor it as real?

Every time we trust, our intuition gets stronger. It's as though it is rewarding us for believing in it. When our bullshit meter works, we go through the world with a secret weapon—the ability to cut to the chase in a split second. Not only are we naturally drawn to what serves us best but also we move through the process with efficiency and speed. Our insight is usually right on the mark, and we follow the inner prompting as though it were a huge red sign with letters spelling "This way."

WHEN YOU ARE CONFUSED, DO NOTHING

When we are confused there is an incongruity between what we are feeling and what we are thinking. Something in our head is telling us to move forward and, at the same time, another equally strong feeling is holding us back. This impasse is not something we need to willfully plow through, but rather a point at which to stop and reevaluate where we are going.

Confusion points the way to a new beginning and will not allow us to take the first path that allays our anxiety. The first path is always the path we know, the way that is familiar and "makes sense." It is very tempting to follow this path, and, if it were not for that nagging inner voice, we would surely go down this road. In addition, most of us are so used to moving quickly that any hesitation is interpreted as a sign of weakness. But we need to slow down and get in touch with what is really going on.

LET IT HAPPEN

When there is a gap between our heart and our head, we become confused. The part that is on automatic is telling us to move ahead, but the part that is coming to consciousness is telling us to wait. This is because we aren't yet ready to make a decision. There are still parts of the puzzle coming together, and, if we act prematurely, we will most likely select a course of action that will not be in our best interest.

The best way I know to deal with confusion is to sit down in the middle of the floor. In a second, the craziness will stop. Maybe sitting on the floor is nuttier than the confusion, or maybe an act so isolated has the power to stop a tangle of feelings and thoughts and bring us back to square one. Either way, the act of sitting recenters us, and we are back in our bodies where we can feel. The feeling is solid and unequivocal and inherently gives us permission to explore the conflicting messages we are getting. We may not get all the pieces at once, but slowly things become clearer. Most importantly, we learn the only time to move is when everything says, "Go!" and not a moment before.

By allowing new feelings to emerge without judgment, we filter and sift new ideas, trying them on for size. We begin to understand that changes take place incrementally and that to rush the process is to invite in confusion. There will be a right time for the change, a way that works for us. There is no timetable for getting clear, only the commitment we make to be real, no matter how long it takes.

From this place, confusion is converted to clarity. We are in sync. What initially produced anxiety is now exciting and becomes part of the grand adventure. Rather than feel apprehensive and out of control, we allow the changes to happen in a graceful way. And, for the moment, we are at peace.

WHEN WE LOVE
IT IS ALWAYS ABOUT US

When we love, most of us think our love is a statement about the object of our affection, the one we love. But the truth is—loving is always about us, never about anyone else. That does not mean that others do not affect us, they do. But they are not the source of love. Rather they serve as catalysts by allowing us to touch our own vulnerability so that we may love.

If we are inspired, it is because we have allowed ourselves to be touched, and if we are overwhelmed with tenderness and compassion, it is because our hearts are open and willing to feel.

We do not inadvertently fall in love. Initially, there may have been an unplanned seductive encounter and a few, perhaps numerous, flashes of euphoria, but eventually the moment passes, and we are left with having to make a conscious decision about loving. No matter how hard we try, we cannot indefinitely stay in an altered state. Inevitably, we are catapulted back to Earth, and the person across from us is "the other." To move forward we need to choose love.

The pain from being pulled apart manifests in many ways, most of them unconscious. We are once again separate, and our first reaction is to pull back, to protect ourselves. Sometimes we strike out and say cruel things, and other times we retreat, barely saying a word. We are not accustomed to dealing with these feelings, and it's hard to understand how something that felt so close now feels so distant. But that is because we forget. We forget why we are here and what we have come to learn.

When we are swept away, we are initially transported to a place of oneness. We have lost our self-consciousness and merged our individual Self with that of another. Together, we have formed a divine union and, for an instant, our separateness has dissolved.

But we are all different, and togetherness does not last for long. We are playing a human game and, in due time, we are apart once again. This is not something that we need to react to—it is simply what happens in mortal relationships. Nothing stays the same. This may be what scares us, but it is also what encourages us to go deeper.

This is the perfect opportunity to acknowledge the division and choose to love the differences.

It is this conscious choice to love that opens our hearts. No one can do this for us, no matter how beautiful or wonderful they are. Ultimately, whom we love is less important than how we love.

When People Are Not Meant To Be Together Anymore, They're Not

We assign reasons for why people are together as though logic could solve the mystery. But the answer is not so much secret as it is enigmatic. Often, deep in dreams, when we are draped leg over leg, two as one, under the goose-down comforter, there, in night's stillness, we intuitively know we are exactly where we need to be.

But this does not mean that we are always ecstatically happy. Feeling good is certainly an option but clarity is what we are looking for here. When we are clear, we want to stay, regardless of how we feel. We are committed to the essence of the relationship and willingly bear its fluctuations. We often fool ourselves into thinking that this feeling has something to do with longevity. But that is not always the case. Sometimes our most profound lessons come from brief interludes—just long enough to change a life forever.

Our commitment is not based on things making sense but rather on a feeling that lets us know we are where we need to be right now. This distinction of "right now" recognizes that what we need to learn and whom we need to learn it with changes all the time. How long we are with someone is not something we can intellectually or physically manipulate. We might convince ourselves that we are with this person for a specific reason, but the truth is that relationships adhere to the laws of physics and energetically have a life of their own.

Like everything else in the universe, each of us has a vibration. This vibration moves at a certain frequency and pulls to us someone who has a vibration that fits with ours. As long as these vibrations remain in sync, people stay together. When they no longer match, people drift apart. Simply said, when people aren't meant to be together anymore, they're not.

I realized the truth of this statement after a couple years of psychotherapy. Both friends and acquaintances frequently commented on how mismatched my husband and I seemed to be. He was very involved in worldly life and I, on the other hand, was much more connected to my inner life. There were problems from the beginning that continued throughout our relationship, but for some unknown reason I chose to ignore them. I tried unsuccessfully to leave the relationship several times, and when I finally did, I never looked back. As the marriage ended in divorce and I heard myself saying we were never meant to be together, I could feel the incongruity.

We had been together and, whether I liked it or not, it was something that was meant to be—if only for a limited period of time. From the outside we seemed so different, but I knew we were vibrating at the same frequency. I pulled him to me just like he pulled me to him. Rather than think the marriage a mistake, I somehow knew it had been a perfect match. We had something to learn from one another, and this was the universe's way of making it happen. The same law of energy that had magnetically drawn us together was now responsible for our separation—the energy had simply vanished.

MEN AND WOMEN ARE DIFFERENT— ENJOY IT!

We have spent most of our lives knowing that men and women are different, but somewhere along the way we decided they were not. In the midst of hailing women's rights, the tables were turned, and we forgot the wonderful variations, the tensions that support and attract, the yin and the yang. In blurring these differences, we have lost the essence of the male/female relationship and interchange, lost the juiciest part.

It is not a fluke that we are born a man or a woman. The body we have is the one we wear, and we are meant to learn certain things while we inhabit it.

Genetically, men and women are different, and the ways they create their lives are gender specific. Men are hunters. They understand the need to go out into the world and bring back the bacon. As women, we are eternally grateful for the plentiful bounty and reward the man by making a loving and nurturing haven. Deep sleep, good sex, and delicious food make the man happy. These things are as basic as breathing and do not in any way diminish the various nuances of a relationship.

The happier and more contented a man is, the more he loves and cherishes the woman. And the more she feels adored, the more she supports his effort. Seamlessly, she is his rock, the underlying foundation that gives him strength and courage.

This symbiotic relationship has perfect equanimity. When we are in tune with our nature, we have a natural rhythm that makes us feel like we have come home. It is both soothing and healing; we are comfortable being who we are and enjoy everything that comes with that.

To respect and honor the body we were given adds a powerful dimension to our lives. When we are truly connected to what it is to be male or female, we routinely pull to us complementary matches that automatically create pleasure and enchantment with the opposite sex. This merging of equal but opposite parts creates a whole that is far greater than the sum of its parts.

The body we take, man or woman, is the layer once removed from the essence. It is as close to the core as it comes, and when we accept that body and all that it means—at that moment, rather than feel trapped—we are set free.

Freedom happens when there is congruence, when we feel one with our skin.

That's why men and women are different. They just are. Enjoy it.

LOVE GROWS
IF YOU'RE NOT IN A COMA

How many times have we heard, "The passion becomes less after you've been together for a while," or "Naturally things are strongest at the beginning"? We buy into these platitudes as though they were gospel, never questioning the inherent nature of love. Time and again, we willingly fall prey to this distorted view and, rather than open up to another way of looking at love, we buy into the status quo. "This happens to everyone," we tell ourselves, "so it must be true."

In the newness of a relationship, we are swept away by feelings that bypass the brain, and we are transported, literally, into another state of consciousness. This happens quickly as our hormones rage. Sexual contact accelerates the process even further. We mistakenly think physical intimacy is real intimacy, and we are shocked when we realize it is not. Although sometimes the initial merging lasts for a while, eventually the disconnection takes place. And when it does, we are unprepared for the pain of separation.

Frightened of our own vulnerability, we pull away. This unconscious retreating shuts us down, and we immediately begin to "think" rather than to "feel." Now we are caught in a trap of protecting ourselves against a false enemy. But it is not the other person who has betrayed us. We have been led astray by our own confused thinking.

The truth is that this is what happens when we don't understand how it really works. We don't get it. We think our opinion is reality, when it just may be our opinion and nothing more.

This static fantasized goal of everlasting pleasure keeps us stuck. We hold on to an idealized notion of what love is, and we get thoroughly sideswiped by anything less. Whatever doesn't fit into our agenda we reject as "not love." We withdraw and blame, and then we regroup, and approach again. We all do a variation of this advance/retreat process—until we stop doing it. The players may change, but the drama remains.

After a while, even we see it. Until we are tired of doing the same old stuff over and over again, we will never change. Unless we are willing to give it up—the story, the illusions, even the hopes and dreams—we can never begin the very real and wonderful process of loving.

An amazing thing happens when we can honestly connect to the monogrammed satchel of stuff that belongs to us, no better or worse than anyone else's, simply ours. The moment we "feel," we stop acting out. We take responsibility for all our behavior, not just the parts we like. We stop getting angry, projecting, and gathering consensus for our point of view. We look at what is and let it be that, regardless of how we would like it to be. We make an actual conscious decision to be present in the moment, so we can "see" clearly. From this space only, we begin to love.

This is not something that just happens to you. You make that choice. By choosing to be real, touching your never-ending well of humanity (the ugly stuff, all of it), you automatically touch the other person's as well. When you love from that place, your generosity of spirit extends effortlessly to another.

To know your Self is to know another, and there is nothing more tender than being known. We do not want to be loved in spite of our humanity, but because of it. When we are loved like that, we are eternally grateful, and joyfully love in return.

We have only one heart. If we close it to hurt, we close it to love. There will never be anything outside us that can guarantee love—not a perfect person, an ideal situation, a signed promise. It is only when we expose our soft underbelly to the universe that we are protected, and the world cannot hurt us. That is the only thing we can be sure of.

The natural evolution of everything is change, movement from moment to moment that encourages us to stay vigilant and not go to sleep. When we stay awake, love grows. It can't do anything else.

BEING HUMAN IS THE KEY TO KNOWING YOUR DIVINITY

—————————— ✿ ——————————

Rather than leave this earthly realm of pain and suffering for a place of perfect peace, the Buddha chose to remain here. He was not deluded—he was enlightened. He could feel so much what it was to be human that that feeling intimately connected him to all living beings. As the Boddhisatva, his infinite compassion sprang from the realization that our common denominator is our human-ness, and it is only through our humanity that we can know God and our true nature.

We can transcend our physical limitations, but we cannot deny them. Our human body, with all its components, adheres to all the laws of nature. I remember someone asking Swami Muktananda about Jesus and the resurrection. "Is it true," they asked "that Jesus ascended to heaven from earth?" "Even a leaf falls from a tree," said Muktananda.

Let It Happen

When we are born as human beings it is not a fluke or an accident. It is the form we take to learn the lessons we need to learn. No matter how much we study philosophy or practice various spiritual disciplines, if this knowledge takes us away from our humanity, it is doing us a disservice.

Truly understanding this life is a result of being real, and we can only be real when we accept our human existence and all that it entails. We cannot decide it is too painful or too ugly and simply go around it. Nor can we decide to exist in some altered state that removes us from life's nitty-gritty. The more we run, the more reality runs after us. For life is everywhere—there is simply no escape.

Every moment we have the opportunity to choose. Our choices determine the quality of our life—our joys, our sorrows. When we put our joys in the accept basket and our sorrows in the reject pile, we are cutting our life in two, never allowing ourselves to be whole. To be whole requires all of it—the good, the bad, and the ugly. Our allegiance must never be to the immediate feeling, but rather to the process, the wonder of being human.

It is only through that wonder that we are able to experience our divinity. Our joy is not simply a momentary high, but rather a solid feeling that anchors us through this earthly existence. We have faith in ourselves, in our own evolution. We are not afraid of being real or of where that might lead us.

As we go deeper and deeper into our humanness, we feel the expansion happening. Each pass fills the heart with joy and creates energy to once again plunge into the human experience. Accepting our life with all its quirks and shady days can set us free.

And at our most human moment, we are truly Divine.

THE UNIVERSE WORKS
IF YOU GET OUT OF THE WAY

Sometimes, things just go our way. We get the job we have been dreaming of, an unexpected check comes in the mail, or things just seem to effortlessly fall into place for no apparent reason. We call it luck or attribute it to simply having a good day, but in truth, we have been given a glimpse of the actual nature of the universe.

We tend to think the timing was right, never realizing that we are an innate part of the process. We are not random recipients of bounty. If only for the moment, our state of being pulls to us this divine experience of synchronicity. There is rhyme and reason to the way the universe unfolds. When we are "in the flow," we have released the illusion that we can protect ourselves by being in control. We have gotten out of the way long enough to experience how effortlessly this process takes place. We must be willing to stop pushing and allow the universe to send us the things we truly need rather than what we keep asking for.

When a bird looks for food, it makes an implicit assumption that it will find the worm and all will be okay. It does not get up and start thinking "What if I can't find food? What will happen to me?" It does not anticipate that there will be a problem. There is an ease with which it moves through its day, an underlying instinct that is minutely in keeping with life's basic nature. It does not think anything. Its being trusts that all will be provided for, and it does not question how.

To be in that state is to observe the precise timing in which all things fall into place and to simultaneously marvel at the exquisite manifestations of an ever-changing universe. When we are fortunate enough to have an experience of this wholeness, we are filled with humility and compassion. We never know when we will be the recipients of such grace—that is part of the wonder.

I never thought a trip to the corner drugstore would deliver such an experience. I had gone there for the sole purpose of buying mascara and found myself wheeling the cart up and down each aisle looking for what else I could buy. On a top shelf, I spotted a box with a picture of a green birdfeeder. I liked the green color, but knew the last thing I needed was another birdfeeder. One had been hanging on my balcony for the past year. It had taken the doves close to three months to find it, but now they came every day. I looked at the box again and put it into my cart. I started to think about why I was purchasing it, and stopped myself. I was just going to buy it, and that was that.

Purchases in hand, I walked through my front door and headed out toward the balcony. There, lying on the ground, was the birdfeeder. My heart stopped. It looked like the wire that had been holding it had snapped. All I could do was stare at the broken feeder. A sense of wonder and wholeness filled my being. I felt disoriented, out of time and space, and yet at the same time I knew exactly where I was. I was 100 percent present. I could feel the intricacy of the process, every tiny little piece falling into place. Feeling it work, I intuitively knew that the birdfeeder had fallen the moment I had opened the door!

The universe operates with speed and efficiency in direct relation to our degree of trust. When we feel stuck, we need to get out of our own way. This does not mean that we simply sit back and do nothing, but rather that we know when to let go, when we have done enough. When we move through the world knowing that we will be provided for, magic happens.

THE BIRD FLIES WITH TWO WINGS— ONE OF DESTINY, ONE OF FREE WILL

❖

The bird of happiness flies with that inextricable mix of surrender and freedom. Surrender is its wing of destiny, and freedom its wing of free will. Without both wings, it is forever earthbound, never able to soar.

With broken wings, we remain tethered to the earth, never experiencing the flight of liberation that comes from allowing both destiny and free will to exist simultaneously. Slicing our life down the middle, we endlessly debate the virtues of both, with the assumption being that one will emerge victorious, and finally, we will have our very neat way of looking at the world. But that never happens. Although eventually we accept one and reject the other, the universe is not that cavalier. It honors both destiny and free will and grants them equal status. By adhering to its governing principle of yin/yang, the universe joins two seemingly opposite points of view and creates something far greater and more magnificent.

Reality Works

To accept that both destiny and free will operate in a life is to see to the core of how things work. At every moment we are living out our destiny and, at that very same moment, with our free will, we are creating a new destiny.

Often, when we are faced with a situation that is out of our control and cannot understand what is happening to us, we say it is our destiny. There is a feeling that we had nothing to do with this—that it just happened. But whether we believe this or not is irrelevant. What matters now is how we deal with what is in front of us. Do we feel victimized and become immobilized, or do we accept "what is" as our own and choose to move forward? The choices we make today, how we deal with our life at this very moment, this is what creates our destiny!

When we see the world from this perspective, we soar. By accepting our destiny, we surrender in a way that has both style and grace. This is not passive submission, but an active yielding that is perfectly aligned with the way things work. We stop flailing at the moon and simply enjoy its many faces. We accept our life as our own.

To be in this place gives us another opportunity to create the life we want. We feel the multitude of options out there and know the power of good choices. Our free will gives us the freedom to move forward in new and exciting ways. When we allow destiny and free will to sit side by side, we enter the interlocking maze that always leads us home.

WHEN FAMILY MEMBERS ARE JUDGED AS FRIENDS, WE'VE FINALLY GOT IT

With a feeling that is stronger than blood and more powerful than genetic coding, we are inextricably linked to our family. Unlike other areas of our life, where we tenaciously cling to rational thinking in the wake of overpowering emotions, our family is perhaps the only place where we willingly abandon logical thinking and lead with the heart.

That is because there is something very real and immediate about family. It does not matter if our feelings are positive or negative, or whether we believe family members are with us for a reason or simply by accident. We are connected to them, and they are connected to us. Nothing can impair that feeling or make it less genuine. Even if we cannot find a deeper tribal meaning, we are left with a feeling we cannot simply dismiss.

Intellectually, we may try to deny the connection, but ultimately it sizzles and sparks and demands that we pay attention. Love them or hate them, family members are capable of pushing every button we have. Criticism from a caustic mother can turn a self-assured daughter into a scared, defensive little girl, and disapproval from a narcissistic father can make a successful entrepreneur feel like a failure. By telling ourselves "it's family," we justify their behavior and ours, and make a thousand excuses for continuing to do things that don't feel right.

But inherent in this uneasy feeling is a way out. As long as we are willing to feel rather than think, we know we are on the right track. The moment we connect to the feeling, we bypass all the "shoulds" and "oughts" and deal with reality, what is right there in front of us. Something that doesn't feel good, in the deepest part of our being, makes us want to leave. We need to listen to that inner prompting and go. For in order to grow and flourish, we must consciously move away from things that don't nourish our souls. And if that includes family, so be it.

Instantly, we reclaim our power. We accept full responsibility for what has happened up till now and know we can choose to change it. We begin responding appropriately. When we are abused, we pull away, and when we are supported and cherished, we love and move close. Here is an opportunity to even the playing field—to choose one another as we would friends.

We have put equanimity in our family relations, and it feels good. We are not talking about a quid pro quo relationship but rather about an open interchange that, on the whole, feels balanced and harmonious. To meet one another in this open and unconditional way creates tremendous possibilities. When family members are judged as friends, the way is paved for lifelong friendships of blood and heart. The script is gone and the rigid rules of interaction have been replaced by a more natural way of being. Finally, family makes sense.

AGENDAS PUSH PEOPLE AWAY

We grow up believing it is always important to have plans, but as much as we love knowing what is going to happen, we never like feeling controlled or manipulated.

There is a very significant but subtle difference between making plans and having an agenda. Making plans requires some necessary forethought—What would you like to do? Where would you like to go? It is about determining what might be a match for the way you feel. Do you want to go camping or do you want to go the movies? The process starts with a feeling and moves out to a specific counterpart to that feeling—movies or camping. When we make plans like this, it is an appropriate way to use our will and create a life that makes us feel good.

Conversely, agendas are at the opposite end of the continuum. If making plans starts with examining a feeling, then having an agenda begins with a conditional thought—if I do this, then I'll get that.

From the get-go there is an implicit assumption that behaving a certain way will produce the desired result. We stay focused on the future, not the present, and do what needs to be done to achieve our goals, regardless of how anyone feels.

Having an agenda is manipulation. When we are the object of someone's agenda, we can feel that we are being manipulated, and it does not feel good. We may not be able to intellectually analyze the interchange, but we can sense the subtle exploitation. Although nothing has been said, we know there is an expectation, a particular way we are expected to be, and intuitively we know it is not okay to say how we really feel.

This "walking on eggs" feeling lays the groundwork for the relationship and sets the pattern for communicating. Almost before we know it, we have bought into this dysfunctional way of relating. We rationalize not feeling good by labeling it "negotiable needs" and proceed to hold back spontaneous thoughts and feelings if we sense they are not in keeping with the silently agreed-upon program. The more we "think before we speak," the more isolated we feel.

Feeling lonely and disconnected in a relationship is the result of being unreal. When we cannot be real, the distance is always palpable. We are acutely aware of the emotional isolation and find no solace in a life that has all of the accoutrements but none of the substance of a real life. With no promise of change, eventually we leave—or worse, we stay.

WE MUST WORK FROM THE OUTSIDE IN AS WELL AS FROM THE INSIDE OUT

We are taught that spiritual life requires an inward turning. In doing so, we neglect another part of life that has equal power to transform us—life's outer manifestations. We are so focused on our inner life that we often become immobilized as we wait for a new feeling to overtake us before we make a change. We are looking for that inner green light. Sometimes, we wait forever and the feeling never comes.

To concentrate solely on one way of changing is to deny the complexity of how the universe works. Energy is constantly moving, and nothing stays the same. If we are to remain vigilant and make good choices, we need to maximize all our options.

If energy creates form, form also creates energy. That is, if what we feel inside is capable of creating certain events in our life, aren't certain things we do also able to alter the way we feel? For example, some of us meditate every day. It's difficult to get up an hour earlier each day and sit, hoping the mind will become quiet. It doesn't feel natural, but we remain disciplined and do it anyway. And then one day our mind stops churning, and we are filled with a sense of equanimity and contentment. Simply the act of placing our body in the same spot every day, regardless of how we feel, has a power all its own. It sends a message of longing to the Inner Self and sets the stage by creating a new form for energy to fill. This newly created vehicle will again connect us to our feelings and take us back to our core.

It is never easy to embrace a new way of doing things even when we know it is in our best interest. Initially, we feel immobilized, and forcing ourselves to do something new feels unnatural. But if we understand how energy works, we realize that it is precisely this feeling that is heralding a change for the better. We are stuck. We have gone as far as we can go without doing something different. Unless we are willing to stretch ourselves and reach out into the world, we will never be able to create new forms to express who we are. We cannot use our inner life as a weapon, retreating from a world that won't let us hide. When we do, we cut ourselves off from a lifeline of possibilities, fresh and different ways to experience the world.

Life is organic. All the pieces fit together with no one part being any more spiritual than any other. Our inner life feeds the outer, and the outer life nourishes the inner. This symbiotic relationship permeates all of life and, until we tap in to that rhythm, our life remains disjointed. No one can tell us when to stay quiet and wait for insight, or when to move out into the world with a sense of purpose and discipline. At each moment, only we can decide how to become more, and what we need to do to get there.

You Can't Spoil Someone With Too Much Loving

ϕ

To call love a quality would in some way diminish it. Qualities are ranked, judged and categorized, some higher, some lower than others. We tend to think of one quality as good and another as bad. Depending on where we rank on any particular day, we can either end up on the top of the quality continuum or on the bottom.

In order to escape this swinging pendulum, let's take a tiny quantum leap (it's really not that difficult) and say we all have a nature. This is basic physics, not anything new. In other words, like all things in this world, we are made of certain stuff, and that stuff is the same in us all. Even though my neighbor and I look different, the juice that put us together is the same in us both.

Now try standing silently next to someone you have nothing in common with. When your mind starts chattering and telling you all the reasons this person is different from you, tell it to be quiet. Just stand there and feel—no thinking allowed. Don't try to do anything other than be next to that person.

If we can shut off the mind long enough, something quite incredible happens. We begin to pick up on the energy—a force field emanating from the person standing there. It's not simply that person's vibration; it's beyond that. A vibration is personal. Much of the time it is used to distinguish one person from another.

This feeling is the opposite of separateness; it breaks down the walls of isolation and goes right to the heart. It is familiar, it is soothing, and it is who we are. This is love, the glue that connects us to one another.

When we love from this place, we heal others and ourselves simultaneously. From this vantage point there is no downside to loving. Taken off the continuum, love becomes a state of being, as natural as breathing. All the manipulative aspects we often associate with loving have been removed, and we are loved solely for our humanness, never in spite of it.

This kind of love never damages, and we can never love anyone too much. When we see beyond the personality and connect at the core, we open up to a world we never knew existed. The more we are loved, the more we recognize the feeling as our true nature. It reinforces what we already know and out of eternal gratitude, we love back.

WHEN WE TRY TO QUIET THE MIND, WE END UP DOING THE OPPOSITE

The mind is like a top. It's spinning so fast it appears to be standing still. It is only when the top begins to slow down that we can begin to experience how fast it has been moving.

It is quite a sobering experience when we first get a glimpse of our frenetic mind. The possibility that it might one day be quiet seems far, far away. Our attempts at meditation have been futile— the mind continues to think and churn out mental images. It seems like the more we try to quiet the mind, the more active it becomes.

That is because, like all things in the universe, the mind has a certain nature. In order to quiet the mind, we first need to know its nature. Just as it is the nature of the leopard to have spots, it is the nature of the mind to have thoughts. Unless we are respectful of that inherent quality, we can never become friends with the mind. We can not bully the mind into submission. When we try to do that, it reacts with a force that is staggering. Trying to push thoughts out of the mind is like saying, "Don't think of an elephant." An elephant is the first thing we think of.

Although it is the mind's nature to have thoughts, these thoughts are nothing more than amorphous images that rise and fall from moment to moment. It is our internal judge that qualifies thoughts good and bad, pure or impure. To the mind, all thoughts are neutral and fleeting. To make peace with our mind, we must surrender to its essential essence and allow it to just be. This is the beginning of meditation, the beginning of peace.

As we sit for meditation, we put aside the inner critic. With eyes open or closed, we simply observe our thoughts. At first our mind chases after this thought and that one; we cannot help feeling attached. After all, it's what we've been doing our whole life! We pretend we are in a movie. We know that what is happening on the screen is not real; neither is this.

Slowly the thoughts stop. The more we sit and watch, without reacting, the more in sync we feel. By making peace with the mind, we have made peace with ourselves.

IT IS ONLY WHEN WE RUN THAT THE CREEPIES RUN AFTER US

Adrenaline starts pumping, and it is our hard-wired signal to retreat. Quite naturally, we move away from things we are afraid of. But what if this instinctual reaction is not always in our best interest? To flee from a rattlesnake makes sense, but what about our imagined fears and perceptions? They seem so real, but are they? What if the further we move away from these fears, the more they gain momentum? Rather than quelling our demons, we are actually fueling them. We give them power by playing their game. To take back our power, we literally have to stop the game.

But how do we stop something that seems so convoluted and feels like it has a life all its own? Feeling is the key to unlocking the door leading out of the maze. There is no shortcut. Unless we are willing to go to that place of vulnerability and feel, we don't have a chance. This does not mean that we should talk about feelings or discuss fears. This is about the willingness to connect in a very real way to the body, not the mind. This entire process takes place below the neck, not above it.

My own experience of this has never left me, even though it happened thirty years ago. The year was 1968, and I was living in New York City on the top floor of a six-floor walk-up. Being alone was my greatest fear, and I avoided it at any cost. I kept myself constantly busy. I worked during the day and had plans every night. Whenever there was a possibility of being alone, somewhere out there in the distance, I could detect rumblings of feelings I did not want to feel. But I felt pretty safe. I had adjusted my life to make sure it was packed to overflowing. None of those feelings were going to get me!

Then one night plans were canceled, and I found myself alone. I could feel my heart pounding in my chest. I felt anxious and was encompassed by an overwhelming desire to flee. I immediately called my friend Ruth and told her I would see her in an hour. There was a winter storm howling outside but that wasn't going to stop me. I hurriedly shut the door to terminal loneliness and catapulted down the stairs two at a time.

I stopped suddenly on the fourth floor landing. As fast as I was running, that's how abruptly I came to a halt. For the moment, I was immobilized, not quite sure what was happening. Then I heard myself saying, "I can't. I can't run anymore." As I turned around and headed back up the stairs, I could feel the onslaught of what was to come.

I never even bothered to turn on the light or take off my hat, coat, and boots. Dressed in full winter regalia, I plopped down in the middle of the floor and said out loud, "Okay, come and get me! I'm tired of running. If you want me, here I am!" Something glued me to that spot. It was as if I were sitting on an energy field and as long as I didn't move I could ride the momentum of what was happening.

As the feelings came, somehow I knew not to fight or try to figure them out, but just to let them be. Sadness and loneliness
enveloped me. I wondered how much more intense the feelings
would become before I was annihilated. I could feel all of it congealing, gaining critical mass. Was I going to implode?

And then something shifted. Just at the point when I thought I
might die from the sheer intensity of the feelings, they peaked and
flipped out the other side. They diminished so quickly, I found
myself smiling. Not only had I survived, I felt like new life had been
breathed into me. There was a moment when I tried to grab for
what had hurt so much, but it was gone. I knew the game was over.
I had stopped running, and the creepies had lost interest.

Today, I still sit down in the middle of the floor and say, "Come
and get me!" It seems to be the quickest way I know to confront the
demons. Besides, I know it works.

Taking Responsibility For Your Life Means Not Fighting With Reality— If It Happened To You, It Belongs To You

It would be nice to know why something happened to us, but can we ever know, and does it really matter anyway? Looking for "why" something happened is a trap we create for ourselves. Even if the "why" satisfies us, we have missed the point. It becomes a rationalization, an escape, and a way of not accepting our life at this moment. What's important is not why the bird ate the worm, but that it ate the worm. Reality is not about the "why," but about "what is." When the "why" becomes the end point, it denies us the opportunity of even accepting a small part of what might belong to us.

Regardless of the event, if it happened to you, it belongs to you! There is no taint of victim consciousness, no excuses for not accepting whatever has come to us. This does not mean that we are personally responsible for what has happened. All it means is that we can't argue with reality, what is right there in front of us. We can still fight injustice or take to task someone who has cheated us, but we need to keep on moving. We have a life to live, and there are things to do. We don't have the time to blame, analyze, and worry.

But how do we move on when something devastating has happened to us? Moving on has to do with accepting our life at this very moment. It means feeling the feelings we often find unacceptable—the raging anger, the gut-wrenching hurt, the intense hate. To own these feelings as our own, regardless of how they came about, opens the door to a new and healing way of looking at our life. It takes tremendous bravery to look at a life that is full of human frailties as well as triumphs and accept it wholly as our own.

Taking responsibility means accepting a life, in total! Whether we like it or not, the life we are living is ours and not someone else's. We do not get to feel proprietary only when it suits us or when things are going our way.

This life is not an accident, not even one, little, tiny part of it. This does not mean that there was not room for improvement or that I might not do things differently from where I now stand. All it means is that I trust the process. The universe delivered, and it ended up with me, not someone else.

HEALING IS A FUNCTION OF CONSCIOUSNESS, NOTHING ELSE

The natural state of the body is wellness. When we are sick, we are out of rhythm with the body's band. This discordant note signals a call to attention, a potent stopping point to reevaluate who we are and where we are going.

Most of us accept sickness, either mental or physical malaise, as part of life. It is true that, being human, we are certainly subject, at any time, to a number of afflictions, but there is a powerful distinction between accepting our humanness and allowing illness to be a constant part of our lives. This does not mean we should chastise ourselves when we are not in top form, but rather that we look at these times with an eye toward discovery.

This is the perfect instant to stop. We breathe deeply and realize there is something very important to learn. We say to ourselves, "I was well, and now I'm sick. What has changed or needs to be changed? What do I need to do, or not do, to once again be in tune with the body?"

Although it often appears that we woke up one Monday with cancer or, out of nowhere, suffered a heart attack, this is not really what is happening. The universe works in very subtle ways and incrementally attempts to wake us up. All illness, regardless of what it is, is a cry for consciousness.

This is a defining moment. How we choose to deal with our illness will continue to lay the groundwork for the rest of our lives. Do we rail at the gods of fate and call our destiny unfair, or do we become stoic and resigned, determined never to question this unfortunate turning of events. Either way, we remain disconnected from our bodies and ourselves, hoping, praying, and believing there will be a reversal. But the turnaround never comes.

That's because only a different way of looking at all the old stuff can trigger a transition, stop the forward momentum. Unless we are open and willing to have no answers for a while, we will never be able to effect a change. Not knowing is the beginning of knowing, and we must pass through this seemingly barren plain, unaware that it holds the fruits of wellness.

By choosing to remain awake regardless of what happens to us, we take control. We resolve to be honest with ourselves, no matter how much it hurts, and to stay connected to the most intimate parts of our lives. Our vulnerability is what opens us, and we are determined to feel no matter how much it scares us. And then we let go, knowing we are not in charge. This is the way we heal.

You Are Always In The Right Place At The Right Time

What is true is always true. We either believe we are always in the right place at the right time, or we do not. We can't have it both ways. When we change our philosophy to fit the circumstances, we are attempting to make sense out of something that frightens us. As our life continues to twist and turn in unexpected ways, we feel compelled to explain its unpredictable nature.

When things go our way, we are gracious. We willingly acknowledge a sense of right timing, a solid feeling of knowing we were in the right place at the right time. But when we are sideswiped, caught off guard, and unable to decipher life's lessons, we rail at the gods of justice and fairness. Bending reality for a quick control fix, we now call it bad timing. Rather than accept what is in front of us as ours, we dismiss large chunks of our life as mistakes. In doing so, we dilute our power and delude ourselves.

Let It Happen

When we know we are always in the right place at the right time, we have tremendous power. We stop wasting energy cutting and pasting fragments of a life that fall outside our imaginary boundaries of convenience. We let the parts fall where they may because we trust the entire process. As each piece intertwines with the next, a montage is created. Colored with triumphs and failures, it is a testimony to our uniqueness and an affirmation of life's wholeness.

To be in this state allows us to create our life from a place of power. We are present—we don't want to be anywhere else. Our peacefulness permeates everything. Some of our experiences are sure to be painful but that does not distort our clarity. We are rooted to life's ever-changing nature. It does not scare us. Rather than run and hide, we eagerly await the next juncture and delight in the presentation.

Finally, we can put our intellect to rest and be in the moment. There is no longer a need to rationalize experiences and manipulate circumstances. We do not have to trust the universe—we trust ourselves. As life unfolds, we get a sense of continuity, of being intricately linked to something larger than ourselves. Intuitively, we know we are not running the show. Moreover, we are not victims of anything—not a fickle universe and not bad timing. Our timing is perfect. We are exactly where we need to be.

WHEN YOU CLOSE ONE DOOR, DON'T OPEN ANOTHER; STAND THERE . . . ANOTHER DOOR WILL OPEN

How many times have we heard, "When one door closes another door opens"? We understand this to mean that two things are happening at once—we have our hand on the door that is closing and at the same moment we are reaching forward to open a new door. As we attempt to corral a piece of the future that is not yet ready to happen, we feel the loss of control.

We are convinced that the only way for things to move forward is to push, to knock open that door. Our self-conscious effort creates a lot of movement but, ultimately, does not take us where we want to be. As we become more anxious, we actually end up pushing away from us what we most want. The universe interprets our fear as lack and refuses to reflect back to us the life we so desperately want.

When one door closes and another door is not yet open, we need to keep our hands at our sides and rest in the gap.

The gap initially appears as a void but that is only because we have nothing to hold on to. In reality, the space between the two doors is where creation happens. This is the place where all the essential ingredients are measured and mixed, where the real magic occurs. A potent brew is in the works and to rush the process is to interfere in the majesty of its wholeness. A steady, quiet vigilance is what's called for, the discipline to wait, watch, and wonder.

This does not mean we are lazy or unprepared. On the contrary, we have done our homework. Now is the time to say, "I have done all I can do. Let it rip!" To realize that we are responsible for all the ingredients but not for the outcome is very powerful. We are left to deal with the stuff we do best—doing what we love— and the universe is left with the creation of the form for doing it. If we can get out of the way long enough to allow this process to unfold, we are delighted beyond our wildest imaginings. The universe delivers a panorama that encompasses it all; possibilities we never even knew existed.

To experience the intelligence of this process is a double whammy! We get a life greater than anything we could have imagined, and we get to live it now! Rather than plan and fret about a life that has not yet happened, we end up smack dab in the middle of one that is juicy and full of promise. When we wait for another door to open, we are letting the universe know we trust it and from that trust, we get what we truly need.

Our Experience Is A Metaphor— Only We Know What It Means

Sitting nude in front of the keyboard should have given me a clue. Initially, it never occurred to me that my nakedness could be a metaphor for my writing. And yet every writing session started and ended quite the same. I would begin fully dressed, removing item after item of clothing as I neared completion of the topic. At the end of each chapter, I was completely undressed. I remember being amused at myself, thinking it was good that I lived alone. Exhausted, I would pick my clothes up off the floor and head toward the bedroom. I was glad this was a solitary project. It certainly wasn't something I could do in public!

Every day, I would sit down at the keyboard to begin the laborious process of culling my psyche. Physically, I was ready. I had showered and put on comfortable clothes. Although I loved this writing process, it was not easy. What was hard was the discipline. Sometimes, I would sit for long periods waiting for just the right words to come. I had done creative things my whole life, but somehow this felt different. I had always felt exposed when doing something new, but now I felt really vulnerable.

What made it even scarier was that I had just closed my art gallery. After six years, the gallery had served its purpose. I could literally feel the energy changing. My decision to close was never conditional—I had no idea what I was going to do but I knew it was time to move on.

Writing was never something I thought about. One day I found myself overwhelmed with feelings and thoughts I just had to get down on paper. Often, in the middle of the night, I would awake and write something. During the day, I would jot down ideas and inspirations. I could feel something congealing but that was as far as I could see. I felt compelled to sit at the computer, even if nothing came out. The discipline was to stay open, to remain connected to my heart and to trust the process. The mere act of writing was healing.

Experience often teaches us in metaphor. There is no book of dreams that can tell us what these things mean. Only we know what something means for us. The process of writing is hard. We write and then we rewrite. Each step requires an unveiling, an unabashed vulnerability. This internal shedding process is a stripping away of illusion to get to the essence. To realize the metaphor instantly connects us back to our heart and our life. Unguarded, we sit naked in our nakedness.

HAVE EVERYTHING AND USE
EVERYTHING YOU HAVE

My girlfriend Marsha is probably one of the most beautiful girls I know and yet, at thirty-five years old, she is still talking about not wanting to be liked for her looks. She has no problem being judged for her brains and hard work; those are fair game, but not her physical beauty. She spends a great deal of time wrestling with her demons and accepting her dysfunctional past, but has been unable to accept and take pleasure from the way she looks, as if there were something wrong with being beautiful. She talks about taking responsibility for her life, but she hasn't quite figured out that her beauty is on equal footing with all the other stuff she has been given.

My friend Paul seems to innately understand this dilemma. Once when he brought in dinner and I asked what I could do, he replied, "Sit there and look beautiful." "No, really," I said. "What can I do?" "Be useful," he said. "Just sit there and look good, that's enough." Every time I went to get up, he made me sit down. After a while, I began to relax. It felt good not to have to do anything to be appreciated.

I remember the feeling that began to encompass me. It was different, something I was not used to. All the ways I gave myself value—I cook, I prepare food, I take care of someone else, I have style in the kitchen—had been taken away. But instead of feeling diminished, I felt cherished. All my grown-up posturing had stopped, and I was like a pretty little girl that was loved by all the boys. There was nothing conditional going on. The feeling was pure and solid—I was confident. I knew who I was and that was enough.

We are so accustomed to trading good feelings and entering into silent agendas with one another that when we just sit quietly in a chair with nothing demanded of us we think we have no value. Most of our life has been spent trying to figure out what we need to do in order to get this and obtain that. We have never gotten the message that it is okay simply to just be.

Once we realize this, we are on to something. Looking at our life from this vantage point serves us well. Suddenly, the whole panorama of who we are is there for the taking. We use it all—recognizing the parts that ease our way, accepting the rest, and rejoicing in them all. Our life is not any better or worse than anyone else's is. It is simply ours. Knowing this truth gives us reverence and allows us to celebrate our humanness.

The universe is abundant and generous. We never need to apologize for wanting anything, and we do not have to prove that we deserve it. Simply by being on this Earth, we are worthy of all life's bounty.

THE VACUUM WILL DRAW IT IN
IF YOU LEAVE IT A VACUUM

Transitions in themselves are difficult. We leave something familiar behind and head toward something unknown. Even if the move was desired, there is always a period of adjustment, a time when things are not as comfortable as they were. We are in flux and not quite sure where we are going.

As familiar props fall away, we enter a rarified zone of unknown possibilities. Before new forms can come into existence, we first must pass through a place without form. This is the juice of the transition. It is here that the vacuum sucks into itself all the things that belong to us. If we are brave enough to stay in this void long enough to allow the natural process to take place, we will draw to us what we need.

This is not merely wishful thinking. It is physics, a law of the universe that is always true. When you want to add something new to your life, get rid of something old. Throw something out, give away clothes, and get rid of the deadbeat boyfriend. The universe will recognize a vacuum, and it will soon be filled.

To understand how it works, we must be willing to stop trying to control the process. The more we panic and hastily add to the empty space, the further away we move from what nourishes our souls. There is a conscious evolution to this transition that will reveal itself in time. This potent period heralds a new beginning, and it is in our best interests to let go and get out of the way.

We may feel afraid, but that is okay. Sure, it's scary when we don't know what is happening, but fear has no power over us when we are willing to acknowledge the feeling, feel it, and do nothing. It is only our reaction to fear that causes us to be impatient and jump the gun. We are so petrified of the nothingness; we create something, anything, to hold on to.

In reality, we are more frightened of being afraid than we are of the actual nothingness. Once we surrender to not having all the parts of the puzzle, we can relax a little. We know we can step in and take charge if need be, but now is not the time. Even though our natural inclination is to do something, we need to do nothing and wait.

To stay in the void takes courage and discipline. The universe has innate intelligence and will automatically create a vacuum out of that nothingness. And left alone, that vacuum will pull to it exactly what we need.

WHEN WE LOVE UNCONDITIONALLY, WE GET A GLIMPSE OF THE INNER SELF

When children and pets love us openly and completely, we attribute this quality to their innocence, never realizing that this love is also our true nature, the nature we have long ago forgotten. This forgetting is not a flaw but an intricate part of the human experience, a chance for us to once again connect to what is real.

For if there is forgetting, there is also remembering, and that is what happens when we are loved in an absolute way. When an animal loves us, there is something familiar about the feeling that makes us feel whole. We do not try to analyze it or question its validity. We accept the love wholeheartedly and readily embrace the feeling as genuine. That is because, without guile or manipulation, our pets love it all. We do not have to be beautiful or rich—we are simply loved for who we are. And because we no longer feel the need to protect ourselves, we can relax and open ourselves up to loving.

When we are loved in this way, there is a direct heart-to-heart connection. In this state of egoless love, we are loved without reservation. Because the other is without an agenda, there is nothing to get in the way, nothing to block the flow of love. All we have is a blank slate, a mirror that reflects our own Inner Self back to us. We mistakenly think the love we are feeling comes from outside us, unaware that we are its origin. It is only when we are loved and love back in this unconditional way that we come to know that it was right under our noses all the time.

This, then, is the beauty of another and what all this loving stuff is about. We need another initially in order to see ourselves. This human game has quite a sense of humor. It has hidden our true nature and dared us to find it. Being loved in this way, we touch the essence of our being and know unequivocally that we are the source, we are the love we feel.

Experiencing this truth, we become brave. Slowly at first, we reach out to love. Having practiced with animals and small children, we are ready for things less safe. Rather than remain separate, we make the first move. Simply because that's who we are, we love another. We want nothing back—no commitment, no soothing words—just the opportunity to open our heart and do what comes naturally.

And along comes love. With heartfelt gratitude, we are loved in return. See, everyone knows everything all the time. Even though intellectually we sometimes can't explain it, we know it anyway. We know how we are loved; we can feel it. It is not something we think about but something we know is real because the Inner Self, which is pure love, is the same in us all. And when we are loved from that place, it is something we never forget.

LEFT ALONE, THINGS ALWAYS BECOME MORE OF WHAT THEY ALREADY ARE

Whether we allow things simply to unfold or we actively seek to make a change depends ultimately on how we feel. Each moment demands we pay attention to the nuance of feeling, so we can decide what to do. There is no blanket answer or quick fix to consciousness. One thing is certain—if we like what we have, we should leave it alone. And if we don't, we should change it.

Many of us make the mistake of thinking that time will make things better. But oftentimes, the passage of time makes things worse. This is because time does nothing but pass. It is neutral and formless, merely open space that forms a backdrop against which our lives unfold.

We are so conditioned to believe in time's beneficence, that we credit this natural phenomenon for major life changes. But in reality it is we, who are superimposed on the divine nature of the ever-changing universe, and not the passage of time, that creates change.

Only we, as the constant variable, can introduce a change and influence the outcome, shifting the momentum.

Sometimes our lives don't work. Nothing goes right, and we suffer mentally and emotionally. This stressful state does not automatically change unless the ingredients that created the situation change. If we wait and do nothing, change will always be determined by what is already there—things will always become more of what they already are.

This is because everything has it own energy field. As vibrations are layered, one on top of the other, momentum builds, creating an aura. This tremendous force field pulls to it all matching harmonious vibrations. This is why, when something is bad, it usually gets worse.

For things to change, we need to choose to move in another direction. We know the old way won't do it anymore, and we are open to new possibilities. Sometimes, we have a powerful realization, but often it is simply a slight shift in consciousness, imperceptible but potent. This newfound clarity instantly halts the forward movement and refocuses the energy, sending it in a new direction.

With this new change, we have an opportunity to observe the process from a different vantage point. Feeling good has its own vibration. It attracts to it feelings that are peaceful and creates circumstances that are expansive and supportive. This time the variables have all come together and created just the right mix. But is there a way for these positive feelings to continue? What can we do?

We remind ourselves that if something isn't broken, it doesn't need fixing. We do nothing and enjoy our moment of grace. What is good does not have to be made better—it will get better naturally, with no help from us. By not interfering in this divine confluence and getting out of the way, we silently manifest energy that reinforces these good feelings and creates new ones.

If we can love ourselves enough and let things be when we are at peace, we will begin to recognize the feeling as real. It is not a fluke or apparition. It is not something we have to cling to, afraid it will be taken away. Feeling whole is our natural state of being, and we have as much right to feel this way as we have to breathe.

FEELING GOOD
IS NEVER CONDITIONAL

We take a job for the money, we date a certain person because we hear they're a good prospect, and we do someone a favor because we want something in return. We live a conditional life, always trying to control what will come to us, because we are afraid that if we don't, we will not get our proper due.

So—we get the money, and the guy, and still we aren't happy.

That is because a conditional life—even if it delivers the desired goal—always leaves us wanting, wanting something more. When we tell ourselves, "If I do this, then I'll get that," we are setting up an equation that we think will result in our happiness. After all, if we did not feel that this would be the case, why would we do it? And yet, time after time, we are disappointed and once again search for new ways to feel good.

So, if happiness is not tied to the coveted outcome, what then is it tied to?

Reality Works

When we stay focused on the present, rather than the future, we begin the process of joyful living.

Focusing on some upcoming event (and never being quite sure when that will be), we live a conditional life where everything is a trade-off. Nothing is ever accepted on its own merits but rather on the basis of what it will mean sometime in the future.

When we take a job we don't really want with the hope of it being a stepping-stone to a job we covet, we will not like going to work every day. When we go out with someone unappealing because we tell ourselves this person is a good business contact, we will not enjoy the evening. Regardless of how sophisticated our rationalizations may be, our inner being will know the difference. We know if we feel good.

A present life is the opposite of a conditional one. It is pulsating with energy that screams, "This is your life now." Its immediacy places us squarely in the moment and makes us feel vital and alive. It is devoid of excuses and, by its very nature, erases any trace of victimhood. Staying present allows us to experience things simply for what they are, without overt or hidden agendas, without manipulation of any kind. We take a job because it is exciting and creative, and, when we get up in the morning, we are glad to go to work. And when we hang out with someone we really like, we feel valued and comfortable and enjoy the company now.

This is what keeps us smack dab in the middle of the action, rather than one step away from it; only this makes us feel intimately connected to our life. When we stay present, we cease living conditionally and enjoy the moment.

Unless we can do that, we will never know true happiness.

WORK IN ONE AREA
DOESN'T GIVE US POINTS IN ANOTHER

There is a common misperception that "living spiritually" entitles us to coast in all other areas of our life. We have assigned a special value to spiritual practices and live as though they had the power to deliver us from our human existence. The more we meditate, astral travel, eat vegetarian food, and remain celibate, the more we feel we are entitled to a privileged life. It is always a shock when we realize that there is no shortcut to a life that works.

After having spent ten years with my guru, I returned to the United States from India. I was now ready for life in the world. My spiritual life was full—my mind was steady, my meditation experiences plentiful, and my understandings solid. It never occurred to me that this richness of experience was just that and not a panacea for my entire life.

It was quite an eye-opener to discover that, psychologically, I was at exactly the same place I had been ten years earlier. It was as though I had been in a time warp. My issues with my father remained, and I had never mourned the death of my mother. Ten years later with all the accoutrements of a seemingly successful spiritual life, I still had not resolved many debilitating childhood problems.

And what exactly was I going to do with my life? The want ads weren't looking for "spiritual sophisticates." I had gone to India in 1970 heeding the call for an inner life, never thinking an outer life would be necessary for a feeling of wholeness.

Starting where I had left off, I began discovering what I liked to do and embraced areas of my life that I had previously neglected. Only by intuitively understanding the enormity of this undertaking was I able to willingly embrace difficult areas of my life.

When we can grasp that all aspects of life have equal value, we are suddenly free from manipulative thinking and deal making with the universe. We don't expect credit in the spiritual realm because we are good parents and providers, and we don't look for points in our emotional life because we meditate. We stop wasting time trying to trade good deeds for unresolved ones. We are able to look at our lives with a critical yet gentle eye. Either we have successfully navigated essential junctures or we have not. And if work needs to be done, we do it.

WHAT IS A PRIORITY AT ONE TIME IS NOT NECESSARILY A PRIORITY IN ANOTHER

Sometimes it takes a long time to figure out the person we want to be with or the new job we want to take. Many of these decisions require intense soul searching and evolve over a long period of time. Often, we inadvertently involve others when we move in a new direction. This happens simply because we are, for the moment, following our gut instinct and, as much as we want to spare ourselves and others of pain, we make the difficult transition because in the end we feel it is in our best interests to do so.

At times we become so focused on the goal that we disconnect from our real feelings. With our eyes riveted on the finish, we are blind to anything in between. We have set our sight on the object of our desire and are determined to achieve that end. It takes tremendous vigilance and courage to acknowledge and change a preset course. We cannot care what anyone else thinks we should do. The same way that we listened to our inner voice telling us what business to open, we need to listen when it says it is time to do something else.

A year before I closed my art gallery I began to feel the energy slowly dissipate. I had learned the art business from scratch—found the artists, put on seven shows a year, became a PR specialist, did my own graphic design—I had never done any of these things before. For me, it was a way to become a part of the community and at the same time learn a business that was aesthetically appealing. For six years I loved and learned from that business, and when I left it a year later I was a very different person.

When I first started to get an inkling that it was time to move on, I went home and cried. For months, every time I thought about leaving, I sobbed. So much had been invested—not just money, but so much energy. Could it be that it had served its purpose, that I had gone as far as I could go, and now it was time for a change?

Once I acknowledged the feeling, I unequivocally knew there was no turning back, even though I wasn't yet ready to do anything. It took me a year to wind down, and the day I finally closed the door, I walked away unencumbered—all my ghosts had been put to rest, and I was ready to go. Afterward, when people heard I had closed the gallery they asked, "Aren't you sad?" "No," I responded, "I cried for a year, and now I'm fine."

The more we trust our sixth sense, the more hints will come our way. We may not want to change something immediately, but for now we have something to think about. Things change incrementally; nothing stays the same. When it is time for a change, we begin to get rumblings. Paying attention to our feelings keeps us connected to our soul's work and enables us to continuously reevaluate the journey.

OUR PERSONALITY
IS THE COSTUME WE WEAR

Getting off the bus in India, I walked into the ashram. The guru in residence was Swami Muktananda, and I was anxious to see what this holy man looked like. I imagined someone with gray hair and a long flowing beard, a soft soothing voice and saffron robes that billowed in the breeze. As I rounded the corner to the back courtyard, I saw a wiry man sitting cross-legged on a stone slab. He was wearing an orange skirt and wildly gesticulating with both hands. His voice was deep and loud, and even though I could not understand the language he was speaking, I could feel how fast he was talking. Everything about him was different from what I had imagined.

Instantly, my mental picture was shattered. He did not have the sedate disposition I had expected. He was larger than life, and his energy filled the room. Standing in his presence, I experienced something quite profound—as large as his personality was, the force of his soul was greater. His personality was simply the outfit he had chosen for this lifetime. This unique costume was not who he was—it was simply what he was wearing.

We all have preconceived notions about how people are supposed to act and look. These beliefs give us a modicum of control; we think we know what to count on, and this initially makes us feel more comfortable. We look for a banker to behave in a reserved fashion, and we expect a holy man to sit quietly and utter profound truths. When what we get is something different, we are thrown off-guard and don't know how to respond.

In order to move forward in any relationship, no matter what it is, we need to let go of our fixed ideas so we can begin to see someone for who he or she really is. This is never easy, for in order to do this, we must accept our own personality with all its idiosyncrasies. The best way to do this is to fix the parts that are dysfunctional and leave the rest alone.

Since there is no blueprint for the ideal temperament, we need to silence all the inner critics and step to our own beat. All of our lives we have listened to other voices; now it is time to listen to our own.

Accepting our nature makes us generous with others. Rather than immediately rejecting things that are unfamiliar, we are not so quick to judge. We begin to enjoy the differences rather than run from them, and the more we delight in our own quirkiness, the more the world becomes a fun place to be.

Partitioning A Life
Is A Game The Mind Plays—
You Have Only One Heart

An invisible tie connects all parts of a life and makes it whole. We may choose to split our life into separate components—home, work, free time, and relationships—but we still have only one life. Life is not just a series of random parts stuck together, but an intricate maze that always ends in wholeness. When we understand this interlocking quality, we approach our life without manipulation.

Manipulation is not always a conscious act, but its effect is the same regardless. No matter what we call it, it is about not being real. As we cut and slice our life into manageable pieces, we mistakenly think we are different in each role we play. We make unconscious deals with all our assorted personalities and falsely assume that our home life has nothing to do with work and that who we are at the office has no bearing on our personal relationships. What we fail to realize is that as quickly as we erect walls that section off our life that's how quickly the universe tears them down. What we do is our business, but it is the business of the universe to show us the wholeness of life, not its separateness.

When we are prejudiced about something, we separate ourselves from others. We may think this is an isolated occurrence, but it is not. We often rationalize how we feel and tell ourselves that this has nothing to do with our personal relationships, work world, or family. But prejudice is powerful. It reverberates to the far corners of our being and takes root. Most important, it closes our heart.

Unlike our obliging mind that grandly creates a false self to suit the moment, the heart is not so nonchalant. Its nature is singular and its integrity inherent. It cannot be split into acceptable parts. At any moment, either it loves or it doesn't. Remember, the heart we are closing to someone else is the same heart that loves our husband, children, and work. To think we can segregate these feelings is to underestimate the efficiency of the universe.

The universe knows it is all connected. So must we. If, in an instant, prejudice closes the heart, that's how quickly loving opens it. Either we have one heart or we don't. And if we do, we need to salute its oneness by acknowledging our own.

WHEN YOUR LIFE IS TOO FULL
YOU RUN OUT OF SPACE TO GROW

Most of us keep very busy. There is no end to the chores and duties, no natural or prescribed stopping point to sit and rest for a while. We overlap our tasks while, at the same time, we complain we have no time to ourselves. No matter how much we do in a day, it never seems to be enough. We are always thinking of new ways to stay occupied and can always find something important to do.

We are taught the value of hard work and use this philosophy to rationalize our compulsive behavior. Our downtime is playing tennis or going to the gym, never just spending time alone. We take our children to school, dance class, piano lessons, and softball all in the same day, and make sure that every minute is accounted for. We pass on to them an unspoken law—keep moving and avoid quiet time at any cost.

Our crazy pace fools us for a while. We interpret the constant movement as a full life and keep waiting to love the life we have created. We think we are moving forward, climbing the ladder, but we keep going in circles, as though one foot were nailed to the floor. We falsely identify ourselves with the things we do and unwisely derive a sense of self-importance from our hectic life. But we become disappointed when our life doesn't deliver. We are unfulfilled and really tired.

We tell ourselves that we don't have the time to do what we want, but the truth is our life does not keep us from doing those things. We do exactly what we want and create a life to satisfy those wants. We may have to care for a sick relative or work eighteen hours a day, but if our need to stay disconnected from our feelings is stronger than our desire to have time to ourselves, we will keep ourselves distracted forever, regardless of the task at hand. This is not a judgment call. It is simply the way it is. We survive moment to moment the best way we can, and if that includes being so busy that we don't have time to feel, so be it.

We do not do this consciously. We actually think we are doing something good for ourselves, but we are not. Our frenzied mind never rests long enough for us to get in touch with our deepest feelings and needs. When we keep every inch of our life stuffed to overflowing, we have no room to grow.

If we sit quietly just for a second, something amazing happens. Out of the nothingness, we begin to imagine and expand. We have created the space and instantly feel energized. We have ceased planning, and arranging and controlling and are instead present, ready to explore new possibilities. For the moment, we have changed the momentum . . . and fed our hungry soul.

THERE IS A WAY THE UNIVERSE UNFOLDS WHETHER YOU GET IT OR NOT

We tend to think there is some inherent power in our worldview simply because it is our opinion. When we hear contrary outlooks, we dismiss them as merely someone else's way of looking at the world. We fail to realize that, regardless of our opinion, or anyone else's for that matter, there is a way things work.

The process of creation, sustenance, and destruction is self-generating. All things are born, live, and die with each stage begetting the next. It is not up for debate and is beyond individual spiritual convictions. When our life flows, it is because our opinion of how it works and the way it really works are the same. For the moment, we are connected to the spiritual underpinnings of the universe and are rewarded with clarity and grace.

But how do we remain watchful and make sure that we are not seduced into adopting popular theories that mentally and emotionally anesthetize us and deny us the opportunity to determine for ourselves what makes sense and what doesn't? How do we create the life we want? Is our opinion simply our opinion, or does it have the power to sabotage as well as create?

The space between what we think and how the universe truly unfolds determines the amount of incongruity in our lives. This incongruity gives us pain and suffering and is in exact proportion to our separation from reality. When there is a wide gap between what we keep wanting and what we keep getting we need to revisit the way we look at things.

The instant we become open to the possibility that there may be another way of looking at the same old stuff, something shifts. We feel the stress and heaviness start to leave. Some pain may remain, but we are not confused. We may not immediately know the answer to a problem, but we feel confident that it will be okay. We have stopped squeezing our magnificent experiences into neatly arranged molds and have allowed them to be real. What remains is a feeling that life works.

When we choose feeling right rather than being right, we move closer to the universal flow. If we are cynical and joyless, it is because we have missed it. We have taken the low road—rationalizing a life that doesn't work and clinging to a philosophy that doesn't deliver. Reality works. It is not something we have to bend or twist to make more palpable. "Getting it" means getting out of the way.

BEING REAL IS BOTH SUBSTANCE AND STYLE

Like a Bach concerto or a Monet still life, being real is an art. It is a combination of both discipline and finesse—the perfect blending that creates the extraordinary. With discipline, we hone our skills to razor sharpness, and with finesse, we create with a uniqueness that is all our own. Combining both, we attempt to forge a life that has both substance and style.

With discipline, we are committed to the act of Self-discovery, and we hold the course, no matter what. We may get weary, but we never lose our resolve. Often when we feel like running, we stay, and many times when we want to cover our ears, we listen. Like warriors till the finish, we remain steadfast.

Discipline is never easy, and it rarely feels natural. It's called discipline because it is an act of will—we consciously put off immediate gratification of our needs and do something that we know in the long run will be of greater benefit to us. We do this because we know we can sometimes be fooled. What often feels most comfortable is not always in our best interest, but merely the way we have always done it. If what we keep getting is not what we want, we need to do things differently. So we employ our will, use our ability to think, and put force behind our decisions when we know we are on the right track. As we sharpen our skills, our minds become quiet. These are the rewards of a disciplined life.

When Einstein said, "God lies right behind a quiet mind," he was acknowledging a force greater than the thinking mind, a power that wakes only when the thinking mind is silent. To experience this power frees the spirit . . . and the essence of who we are rises to the surface and begins to bubble. Like a geyser waiting to explode, we are pregnant with possibilities.

A still mind is the bedrock of creation, and it is here that we ply our craft. If we are able to stay in the silence for even just a short time, we are graced with a fresh peek at life. Looking from this angle, we have dramatically changed our perspective. We are no longer limited by what we previously thought was possible; we have just enlarged the vista.

This is the moment that finesse kicks in and gives us an opportunity for an artful life. Finesse is the dance of style, the human quality of uniqueness waiting to express itself. Sitting firmly on the mind's stillness, it reaches to the far corners of the universe and creates with bold strokes. It says, "There is something special about me, and I am eager to see what it is."

Sitting on solid ground, we reach for the stars.

BECOMING LESS—NOT AN OPTION

Beginning relationships have such promise; we vow to allow one another the space to grow and flourish. To be the most that we can be—that is what we want. The openness we initially experience sets the agenda; we expect to be loved and cherished for who we are, and anything less is unacceptable. We bathe in the ease of being understood and breathe easy—finally we are home.

We become so accustomed to just hanging out that we are taken aback when the communication breaks down. There seemed to be such a natural pairing, an acceptance of one another that was easy and comfortable. We remember when anything that came out of our mouths was good enough, a way of being that was both playful and spontaneous. But over time, we have become self-conscious, afraid to talk without first thinking, measuring each word we say. We feel agitated and confused, and what was once delightful is now tedious.

Although we are not quite sure of the problem, we want to fix it. What feels so bad? we ask ourselves. What happened? We are willing to negotiate, to change our behavior, and do whatever it takes to alleviate the pain of isolation. We are tired of being misunderstood and weary of explaining our every move. In our need to be known and loved for who we are, we make a mistake, and compromise our essence.

We agree to become less intense, less opinionated, less everything. Whenever we hear "You are too much for me" or "You are so clear about what you want, it makes it difficult for me to say what I want" these are red flags, clear indications of a mismatch. Rather than take these comments personally and feel there is something wrong with you, you need to remember who is speaking. You are being given information about the other person—that person is telling you something about him- or herself.

When people have trouble holding their own, rather than rise to the occasion and become more, they often want you to become less.

Now compromise is a good thing when we are talking about whether to go the movies or go dancing, but it is never a good thing to compromise on essence. When we do that, we tell ourselves to tone it down, to stop saying how we really feel, to become something less. We so much want to keep the relationship that we shut down in the real, physical world for the hope and dream of being open in the ideal one. We are afraid that if we are true to ourselves, real and fully alive, we will scare the other person away. So, we willingly diminish ourselves to quell our overwhelming fear of loneliness. But being unreal is always lonely, and in the end we are more isolated than ever. We may have lost the other person, but more importantly, we have lost our Self.

LET IT HAPPEN

We are willing to make changes in our behavior, but they must feel true. We can be accommodating, as long as we are not squelching our spirit, and we will change because it is good for us to change, not because we are "trying" to please someone else. When we "try," we become less, and that is never an option.

VISUALIZING WHAT WE WANT ALWAYS CUTS US SHORT

Most of us walk around with an idea of what we want. We have very definite specifications and actively look in the physical world for the mental pictures we carry with us. We have a laundry list of qualities, characteristics, and traits we feel we cannot do without, and in our minds, they add up to the dream job, the perfect mate, the ideal situation.

But even when these dreams become our everyday life, they never seem quite enough.

We are encouraged to be more and more specific and hear repeatedly the need to focus on the goal. Inherent in this proclamation is the assumption that what we choose to concentrate on comes to fruition, and that what we say we want, we truly want. For while it might be true that we can use our will to create the situation we desire, it is also true that what we end up with just might not be all we thought it would be.

LET IT HAPPEN

As we visualize what we want and that mental picture becomes more crystallized, we actually reduce our opportunities for satisfaction. The more rigid we are with our terms, the more we limit the possibilities. This is because we can never think of all the pieces, never solve the entire puzzle.

We focus on what screams the loudest—our preprogrammed desires rush to the surface and demand to be satisfied. Our perfect man has dark hair and light eyes, and our new job pays us more money than we have ever made. The universe delivers to us exactly what we have asked for and no more. Our fixed agenda has left out the subtleties of life, the missing parts that make us feel whole.

Have you ever wondered what it really means when someone says, "It happens when you're not looking"? This statement is not merely glib commentary on coupling, but a profound truth that goes right to the heart of the matter—when we are not rigidly focused on a specific form, we begin to notice all the possibilities around us.

This does not mean that we give up our dreams, but rather that we cradle those dreams softly, giving them room to grow, expand, and, if need be, change. We still need to visualize, but with a yielding quality. Centered in the heart, we hold our vision and at the same time loosen our grip.

The universe instantly responds to this shift. We begin to see things we have never noticed before, people and situations we have never even thought about. We have just increased our odds.

HOLD THE FEELING,
NOT THE THOUGHT

––––––––––––– ⚙ –––––––––––––

For most of our lives, we are concerned primarily with our physical reality. If we can see it, if we can touch it, then it exists for us. We are taught to think, rather than to feel, and are told that dreaming, for the most part, is a useless pastime. Our world is grounded in the concept of matter, and we are rewarded for being practical and logical. We go through life holding strong to this belief and get plenty of support along the way.

So it comes as somewhat of a surprise when we realize that things may not be as concrete as they appear. As we come to understand that the world exists on many different levels—the physical world being simply the most obvious—we open up to new ways of creating the life we want. Our black-and-white world enlarges to multiple shades of gray; what we believed was possible suddenly expands. We begin to experience the power of our thoughts and realize that if we can imbue these thoughts with enough positive energy, then they just may manifest on the physical plane.

The feeling is exhilarating, and we feel powerful. We have stretched the boundaries of our perception and tapped in to special knowledge, gotten an edge on the competition. We concentrate on what we want, meditate on it, and write affirmations. We become consumed with our idea coming to fruition and press on, no matter what.

And then it happens. We get what we want. The process may work, but does our life? This is the question we need to ask ourselves.

After all, the will is very strong. If we apply all our energy in a tightly focused stream, there is a great likelihood we will be successful; our thoughts will become our reality. But unless we get a "match" (a fit with who we are), we will never be deeply satisfied. We may get the form we think we want, but the essence will be missing. There will be an initial burst of euphoria (we have reached our goal), but that is nothing more than a passing gratification; it will not sustain us or nourish our souls.

Thinking of our ideal man, we hold an image of someone tall, blond, with a full head of hair. We make the picture even more specific by "seeing" no children and a big house on the water. We believe that the more detailed we become, the closer we get to what will make us feel good, but actually, that is not correct.

The more we hold a specific image of what it is we want, the less we are able to recognize what truly belongs to us. Our fantasy sidetracks us and blinds us to other possible matches. If our Mr. Right is standing next to us, short, dark, and balding, we miss him.

Rather than hold a thought, we need to hold a "feeling." If we want to be loved and cherished by someone, we need to ask ourselves, "What does it feel like to be cared for?" Once we connect to the feeling, we have a home base.

This means that unless that feeling is there, we are not interested. This is the starting point. We stop attracting men who are tall, blond, and wealthy, if they are not capable of loving. We are not naive; we are not expecting instant love, but rather a solid beginning that has limitless possibilities.

Once we are able to let go of the mental image (the thoughtform) and concentrate on the feeling, we begin to create a life that works. We stop working at jobs we thought we wanted or staying in relationships we thought would "be good for us."

Opening up means opening up. As long as we stay focused on the feeling, the rest is up for grabs. Does it really matter how someone looks if we are turned on and happy? Isn't that what it's all about anyway?

WHEN YOU MISS THE SIGNS AND SIGNALS, THE UNIVERSE UPS THE ANTE

Every one of us has an inner voice. It is not weird or accidental that sometimes we hear it. Sometimes it is loud, sometimes soft, but always, it has our best interests at heart. Our problem is not with the quality of that voice, but with our ability to recognize it and accept that it is real. When we are connected to our inner voice we have the edge, the tool to accurately interpret the messages we receive.

This is not about analyzing information but rather staying open to clues the universe might deliver. Just because we can't figure out why something is happening is no reason to assume that it has no meaning. Life is never quid pro quo; only we can figure out what something means for us. If we slap someone and that person hits us back, we immediately understand (and accept) why this is happening. But what about a freaky car accident or a perfectly healthy person's heart attack? Accepting your life does not mean throwing up your hands and assigning a random quality to it. Either we are connected to all things or we are not, and if we are, then the things that happen to us have meaning.

Things sometimes happen in a certain way, a sequence of events unfolds, and we find ourselves saying, "What's going on here?" By wondering this we are acknowledging a feeling. Perhaps it is that inner voice, giving us a nudge, suggesting that we take a deeper look. Sometimes, it's nothing more than a speeding ticket or a flat tire, and sometimes it is catastrophic. Have you ever bothered to ask someone who's had an unexpected heart attack if there were any strange occurrences leading up to it? Whenever I have asked, the person has always remembered a series of out of the ordinary incidents that he chose to write off as "accidents." These seemingly disparate events are, in reality, connected. They are the signs and signals we so often overlook, the signposts that announce the twists and forks in the road, the universe trying to deliver its message. Every time we miss it, the universe ups the ante.

A good friend of mine, a physician, spent two years talking about taking time off to reassess his priorities. (It was obvious that they were out of whack and not making him very happy.) He used his busy schedule to make extremely reasonable excuses. Within a four-month period, he had a car accident, kidney stones, a fire in his office, and triple bypass surgery. Lying in bed, unable to move and forced to take a sabbatical from his practice, he finally realized that this was the universe's way of giving him what he truly needed. He needed quiet time, a chance to slow down his racing mind, and this was the form that was capable of delivering the message, a message he chose not to listen to for two years.

The inner voice not only tells us once what we need to hear, it nags us. If we don't get it, don't make the necessary changes, it comes again in a different form. There is no end to the mutations and permutations of experience. They are as endless as the people who create them and, in the universe's infinite wisdom, are precisely suited to the recipient. Every time we miss the silent whisper, we miss a chance to shift in a fluid way. Listening to the inner voice doesn't remove life's obstacles; it just makes the whole process a little smoother.

We Are Naturally Elegant When We Are Focused

On the most mundane level, elegance means the ultimate in sophistication, the epitome of fashion. When we call someone elegant, we are referring to the artistic way a person presents him- or herself and the effect that presentation has on others. We are enamoured— that individual has style. But this type of polish is fleeting, for it is dependent on outside props. If we have a bad hair day, are we no longer elegant?

True elegance is not possible unless it is intimately connected to the Self, that is, it does not matter how good the outside looks unless it is congruent with the inside. Being beautiful only carries us so far—we must also feel beautiful.

Each of us has a place inside that feels like home. It is different for us all, and no one can tell anyone else where it is. We figure it out by being brutally honest with ourselves, by being brave enough to accept the truth, whatever it might be. This rawness anchors us to what is real and keeps us focused. We are centered, and this unity is elegance in action.

When we are focused, there is a point of convergence where all the rays intersect. This juncture of energy is our place of power. For example, if we put our inner critic on hold and accept all our feelings as valid, regardless of what they are, at some instant they all become part of the same group. They now have a cohesiveness, a compatibility, whereas a moment before they were incongruous.

When we choose acceptance over rejection, we get wholeness. We are no longer splintered. We have stopped fighting internal demons and started using our energy in a more productive way.

This feeling of completeness is the result of being balanced. We are not talking here of a quid pro quo arrangement with four items in the plus column and four equal items in the minus column. True serenity is homeostasis, a poised internal state that holds all the elements equally, allowing each of them to be what it is. This does not mean that we close our eyes to the issues that need resolution or to qualities that need repairing, but rather we recognize this as our life's work—there will always be something to fine-tune.

By surrendering to the whole gamut of our humanness, we have made room for it all, even the stuff we have the hardest time accepting. This equanimity is solid, and its firm foundation keeps us focused on the Inner Self.

Using this foundation as home, we round the bases with grace, style, and natural elegance.

I Am Not Afraid Of Things That Scare Me

— ⚙ —

When someone tells us that he or she is afraid, the natural assumption is that that person is immobilized and cannot act. Fear has a way of stopping us dead in our tracks. Something pushes the panic button, and the process stops. The sad part is that the result is not merely a stop, but a "reversing," as all forward movement comes to a halt and we retreat to a place of security and comfort.

For the moment this might satisfy us, but eventually we are once again faced with the same fear. For what is in darkness always comes to light. The energy we expend pushing this feeling away from us ultimately becomes the force that pulls it back.

But what if we changed the paradigm of fear? What if instead of shutting the door on fear, we welcomed the ominous feeling as a messenger of change, heralding the possibility of newfound happiness? What if feeling the feeling were actually different from reacting to the feeling?

To move through fear to the other side, first, we must be brave enough to feel afraid. But that is not enough. We need to feel what scares us, while at the same time disciplining ourselves into not reacting in the old familiar way. This takes tremendous courage and willpower and is a perfect place to exert one's will. If we can succeed in changing our hard-wired way of responding, we will be able to experience fear from a new vantage point.

Holding two seemingly contradictory feelings at the same time is the key to navigating this crucial juncture. We stay in touch with the feeling of fear and experience it as a vital insight into our psyche. This look shows us what we need to work on, where we need to focus our attention. Looking at fear from this perspective changes everything.

Rather than move away from things that scare us we now move toward them. Inherent in this feeling that frightens us is the possibility of freedom, and to enjoy the paradox is to see to the heart of things. The juxtaposition of these feelings forms a gestalt that allows us to see fear as a beacon that lights the way to the understanding of one's Self. Most important, we welcome the opportunity to go deeper.

As we embrace the feeling and relish the chance for change, things begin to shift. As long as we are able to exist in a state of feeling that has no definitive answers, we break the boundaries of a constrained life. And because we know that things do not disappear immediately, we surrender to the incremental process of being real moment by moment.

Simply by staying put and welcoming an uncensored life, we reclaim our right to joy.

WILL IS ABOUT MAKING CHOICES NOT MANIPULATING OUTCOME

Each of us has a personal force. This force goes out into the world ahead of us and forges our reality. This energy is malleable and has the ability to create as well as to destroy. As we watch changes take place, we realize the power of our will and what it can accomplish.

As children, we are always testing boundaries. How far can we go? How much can we push? Oftentimes we go right up to the edge, wanting to go just a little bit more. Once we get the parameters straight we are usually okay, but we never stop exercising our option to go further.

This is what makes it so exciting. There is no limit to the ways we can use our will to create what we want. The more we want something, the more tenacious we become. We push ahead, no matter what signs and signals we get along the way, and in the end we achieve the goal.

Let It Happen

Face to face with our creation, we have an immediate sense of satisfaction. We are pleased with ourselves and that ego boost momentarily sustains us. But it is not long before that initial high subsides, and we are left with the mundane reality of what we have created. We ask ourselves, "Is this what I really want?"

Now the real work begins. Backtracking is not so terrible as long as we can keep connected to what feels right. No one can tell us this, and nothing is cast in stone—we do it till we get it right.

Only by letting go of the goal and focusing on the present moment can we access these feelings. Once again, we summon our will but this time with a more gentle hand. Rather than use it to block all opposing information, we use it in a more fluid and productive way. Moving out into the world, we ask for information (no matter what it is) that will help us. If what we get is not what we want to hear, we listen anyway, knowing this information is meant for us.

Once we make the decision not to use our will to manipulate outcome, we are on solid ground. And as we let go of our fixed timetable, things begin to rock and roll.

Magically, we begin to get new and exciting pieces of the puzzle, information we never knew existed. At the most unexpected times and in the strangest places, we hear what we need to hear at precisely the right moment. We accept it all and refuse to filter the parts we don't like.

By relinquishing control, we have kept our soul's power intact. Our will is no longer in the service of our ego but responds instinctively to our deepest needs.

WHEN WE ARE VULNERABLE, WE ARE PROTECTED

We often associate being vulnerable with being afraid. There is a negative connotation to the word; as a result, most of us avoid this unguarded position at any cost. We tend to think of it as a liability or a handicap, but in truth, this exposure creates the opportunity for growth and, ultimately, peace.

Two years ago, I had three auto accidents in one year. None of them were my fault and no one was hurt, but they scared me just the same. The first one was a small bump in the supermarket parking lot as I was pulling out. I wondered why it had happened—the other car appeared to have come out of nowhere. The second time I was hit from behind as I waited at a light. The third time, a car going about sixty ran a red light and hit the front of my Explorer, sending me careening off the road.

All of these "accidents" disturbed me. I simply could not dismiss them even though, legally, they were not my fault. I never thought of myself as a victim and innately knew that somehow I was part of the equation. I could feel a pattern building—each accident was more serious than the last; the universe kept upping the ante. I spent a year trying to figure out what was going on, and I came up with many explanations, but none of them gave me that feeling of resolution. I could feel the universe trying to teach me something, but I just couldn't get it.

Then, one day as I was driving along, not thinking of anything, it came to me—I had thought I would never have an auto accident. In my arrogance, I believed the things that happen to most people couldn't happen to me. I had deluded myself into thinking that my spirituality protected me and that moving through the world accident-free was my reward. In my desire to be special, I had mistakenly left my humanness behind and, in the process, become cut off from others.

Instantly, I understood the lesson—separateness leaves us unprotected, disconnected from the divine energy that runs through us all. What happens to one of us is a possibility for us all. Accepting our humanness, with all its imperfections, makes us vulnerable and once again connects us to the source. This is what protects us. Only this.

WORKAHOLICS
MISS ALL THE ACTION

We embrace our work with passion and devotion, willingly sacrificing family and friends. We believe that the longer and harder we work, the more we will be rewarded. Ostensibly, our focus is on money and prestige, but in truth, we do these things because we feel they will make us happy. But do they?

No matter how overwhelmed we become, our minds and bodies racing, we make excuses for our hectic life. "This is what I need to do to get ahead." "My job demands I work these long hours." We tell ourselves these things because we need to believe they are true.

After all, we spend the majority of our life at work, and to admit that there is something wrong means we have to stop. And stopping is what we don't want to do. We purposely keep ourselves overloaded with grueling schedules and constantly ringing cell phones. We are so used to not feeling that we keep ourselves distracted with this overpacked life; for to stop would mean to feel, and this is what we are subconsciously avoiding.

This automatic existence robs us of feeling—of being present—and keeps us, always and forever, removed from the action. Our glamorous busy life has failed to make us feel good.

That's because, to feel good, we need to feel, period. But that's not possible if all our energy is above our neck. A racing mind prevents us from feeling and keeps us from experiencing joy.

To stop this runaway train, we need to recognize that we are on overload. Rather than do more, we need to do less. If we keep pushing past this point, we will feel even more overwhelmed. This is when we get sick, make mistakes, have a fender bender. We begin to get little signs and signals from the universe telling us to slow down. And if we don't listen, the message keeps getting louder and louder.

I knew an attorney, who kept saying he needed to slow it down. He wanted more time with his family, more time for himself. He was literally on a roller coaster from morning to night. And then, after saying the same thing for many years and never doing anything about it, he had a massive heart attack. He was young, in his early forties, but it stopped him in his tracks. He was confined to bed rest for a month and not allowed back to work for two. When I talked to him he told me he "knew" the attack had saved his life, given him a chance to do it right.

You do not need a heart attack to get it. You just need to stop.

But how do we stop when we are going a thousand miles a minute?

The quickest way is to sit on the floor right where you are. This immediately bypasses a frantic mind and grounds you. I do not know if plopping on the floor is so physically ridiculous (I've been known to do this in full business attire) that you are instantly refocused, or if sitting immediately centers you in your body and takes you out of your head. Either way, it stops a racing mind and allows you to breathe.

Breathing, we become calm. This is because for the moment, the mind is at rest. Feeling our body, we stop the constant chatter and listen to our beating heart. Now we are present. We are the action.

At least we have a starting point.

Real Sexuality Is Not About Sex

⚙

When we talk of sexuality we are not talking about explicit sex, either in word or deed. Rather we are referring to a gut feeling that bypasses the mind and body parts and stimulates all the senses.

Have you ever noticed the lack of self-consciousness and the confidence that someone really sexual exudes?

That's because real sexuality has nothing to do with thinking; it has to do with being—being alive, feeling connected to an inner core. When we are allied with our Inner Self we are turned on and when we are turned on, people are turned on to us.

In the classical literature of Kashmir Shaivism, kundalini is Divine energy, the snake that lies coiled at the base of the spine. Uncoiled, it moves up the spine, where it reunites at the top of the head with God, the Divine, and your own true Self.

As this energy is released it creates a vibration that is very powerful. This vibration is an emanation of the Inner Self and moves with strength and speed in the physical world. When we are in the presence of someone whose kundalini has been awakened, we pick up a different pulsation; there is something very attractive and engaging about this person.

Most of the time we have no idea intellectually what is going on—we just feel attracted. Initially, we may think the attraction is sexual, but that is just how we have previously interpreted wanting to be near someone. Now, all of our senses are stimulated, and we are awake, aware of a different energy that is both intoxicating and alluring.

This force captures us, and we are inexplicably drawn to the juicy feeling. We feel the need to move closer and closer because the energy is familiar; it may be the other person's but it is our energy too, Divine energy, the same in us all—and when we feel it, we know it. We cannot help but respond. With the other as a mirror, we are drawn in, never realizing we are turned on to our own vibration.

Feeling whole, we glow from the inside. This is what real sexuality is all about.

WE HAVE ALL THE TIME IN THE WORLD AND NOT A MOMENT TO WASTE

Getting it right takes time. There is no shortcut to consciousness. Often the path is tortuous, sometimes smooth. Each twist and turn adds polish to the rough-cut diamond. We are gems in the making, and how intensely we shine depends on how regally we play.

To be a real player takes courage. We have to embrace our life as our own and fully participate at every moment. Many of us look like players but we are simply going through the motions. We have learned what to do in order to look like our lives have meaning. But even with all the accoutrements of a successful life, we still don't feel vital and awake.

That is because aliveness is a function of essence, not of form. To feel alive, we must decide where to put our attention and how to spend our time. Unless we are willing to go for what nourishes our soul, rather than for what satisfies our head, we will never connect to that essence. Ultimately, where we choose to focus our energy determines the quality of our life.

Reality Works

Any situation can be the starting point for being real. We manifest that opportunity in everything we do, regardless of the people or circumstances. As our life unfolds in front of us, we make choices, and these choices set the ground rules. They determine the playing field and the players—whom we keep close to and whom we move away from. How we choose either opens the way to essence or closes it.

Our timetable must always be our own and serves us best if it is open-ended, a limitless backdrop for choices to reverberate against, allowing us to determine what feels true for us. We do it till we get it right—that is the commitment we make to ourselves.

We may not be able to change another person's way of looking at the world, but we can surely decide whether we want to be around that person or not. Either we grow and flourish in someone's company or we do not. This is not just about feeling good, but about feeling genuine. And since feeling real is the barometer of the Inner Self, the less conditional we make the choice, the better. Stripped of all "what ifs," we choose from the heart, able to commit to life and wherever the path might lead us.

This is why we have all the time in the world to do it right and not a moment to waste with something that is manipulative and devoid of essence. Our life has depth because we are willing to touch it. Without judgment, we unequivocally accept responsibility for the choices we have made, and know that, if need be, we can make new ones.

Suddenly doors open. A kaleidoscope of opportunities reveals itself. No longer confused, we are ready for the changes that are to come. We are confident that they are just perfect for us and that we are perfect right back.

You Don't Get To Rest
But You Can Be Comfortable
With What's Going On

We spend so much of our life asleep, that when we do finally wake up we have a tendency to overstimulate ourselves. We are so afraid of once again dozing off that we create a life that is constantly churning. While this movement makes us feel alive and vital, it also develops a drama in which we star. With something always going on, we get to have a story, an excuse for why our life is not yet happening. Stuck in this story, we have trouble seeing things as they really are.

In order to see clearly, it is important to understand the difference between conscious watchfulness and obsessive observance, for without this differentiation we make the mistake of thinking that the goal is to evaluate our every move with a microscope. We become so minutely aware of every thought and gesture that we actually lessen our awareness rather than increase it. To see to the core of anything requires detachment, and we need to let go long enough to get a good perspective. Sitting so close distorts reality—we need some breathing room.

You don't get to rest (no going to sleep), but you do get to breathe deeply and feel good about yourself. Inner work is not a six-week, seven-step program. Once you make the decision to wake up, you are on the train. It doesn't matter how many stops the train makes—all that matters is that you are on it.

Sometimes we ride a wave of grace and learn the first time from our mistakes, and at other times the train is so slow that we think we will never get to the next stop. But eventually we always move out, on to another adventure, another stop along the way.

Being comfortable with the stops is as important as loving the movement. It all works together in a symbiotic process designed to make us whole. The stopping allows us to consciously observe with a gentle eye, and remain vigilant regardless, while the movement lets us know that nothing stays the same. We have made an inner commitment to stay awake and that gives us courage and strength.

Each of us has our own inner clock and no two people are alike. We cannot look at anyone else to determine how we are doing. If we look for kudos from anyone, we will be disappointed. As we listen to our own inner voice, we let go of our fixed timetable and surrender to the natural process of wakefulness.

Giving ourselves permission to relax, we sit back and enjoy the ride.

YOU CAN WANT SOMETHING ELSE
WITHOUT KNOWING WHAT IT IS

Unaware of its source, we are sometimes anxious and discontent; nothing feels right. It's a free-floating feeling, one we can't seem to pinpoint. We don't hate our job, but we really don't like it either. Our relationships are okay, but none of them are close and intimate. We go through all the motions but still feel disconnected from ourselves. The most we can ask is to be attuned to these fluctuations and see if they have any staying power. What's really going on?

Because we don't have the answers, we mostly disregard these feelings as irrational, hoping they are fleeting and will pass. But they linger, and eventually we must either rationalize or confront them. After all, we ask ourselves, if we don't like what we are doing, why don't we do something else? If we don't want to be with this person, whom do we want to be with? Could it be that what works for us at one time simply doesn't cut it at another?

Reality Works

The right question to ask ourselves is this: Do we have to know what we want in order to know what we don't want? And if we know what we don't want, does that move us closer to the things we need?

Knowing evolves in steps. We do not wake up one morning and have all the answers. Often, we learn about ourselves through a process of elimination. Like peeling an onion, we strip away layer after layer until we get to the good stuff. Not this, not this, we say, as we get closer to what feels right.

If truth be told, most of the time we have no idea where we are going or where we will end up. It doesn't matter. What does matter is that we are leaving behind what doesn't work, what we no longer need. As long as we can let go of broken dreams and worn-out goals, we can move in a different direction, one that nourishes our soul. If we are fortunate and grab a bit of grace, the minute we let go of the old way, something new and interesting comes along. But that is usually not the case.

This shift is never easy, and we usually land in limbo. We are between two doors—one that has closed and one that is not yet opened. If we wait until we have all the answers we will never move out from that deadly secure place. We may be afraid, but that is never a reason to stay stuck. Fear of the unknown is natural. We move forward by acknowledging our fear and accepting the discomfort as part of the process.

By staying connected to our feelings, we remain vulnerable and open to unimaginable opportunities and possibilities. And by identifying our excess baggage, we have lightened our load and increased our chances for happiness.

BEING REAL
MEANS BELIEVING IN
YOUR OWN GOODNESS

We cannot be real unless we love ourselves, and we cannot love ourselves until we believe in our own purity of heart. This is not about something we do, but rather about something we are. It is unequivocal, our natural state of being—the opposite of sin, the same as light.

As long as we remain disconnected from that innate goodness, we can never be genuine. We will always be one step from the good stuff, always pushing away the joy that comes from an accepted life. Anything short of loving it all misses the mark, and we are left with only a shadow of substance. The shadow taunts and teases us, yearning to merge with the true Self.

Our real Self is there for the taking—ripe—waiting to be loved, waiting to be forgiven.

Forgiving ourselves begins the task of recognizing the goodness. True forgiveness has the power to set us free. It is never a blanket absolution without responsibility, but rather an opportunity to fully accept ownership of our deeds, to bestow the same compassion on ourselves that we would on others, and finally to move on. Without forgiveness, we are forced into a world of intellectual rationalizations and mutated forms. We end up creating a life that fits the punishment we think we deserve. We have done something bad, and this is our payback. We don't deserve to be loved.

But we have already been punished. We have punished ourselves. It is now time to let go. This life is not about retribution. True, there is an ebb and flow, but it is not about keeping score. We are allowed to make mistakes, to try again, and even to make the same mistake twice. There is no time limit. We do it till we get it right.

When we trust the process, the process unveils the ways to love. This is where we get to exercise our will. We can choose to connect to our essence and what it is to be human with all its fits and starts, or we can twist the love into a shape that fits our vision of a punishing universe. Either way, we draw to us what we feel and create a life from those feelings.

But that is not the end of it. There is truly a way that the universe works, whether or not we get it. And when we are in sync with that way, we are in the moment, absolutely real. Staying rooted in the purity of the process, we exude a quiet confidence that allows us to be totally ourselves and to open up to life. We trust our instincts and give ourselves plenty of space to express all that is to come. Without agendas or manipulation, we move through the world okay in not knowing what will come next. We dare to be vulnerable, and that rawness instantly makes us real.

ONCE YOU KNOW YOUR OWN STUFF,
IT'S ONLY STUFF

When T. S. Eliot spoke of ending up where you began and seeing that place as if for the first time, he was talking about the characteristics of stuff and the poignancy of the self-discovery process. It was his way of saying that this work is never finished, but something we revisit again, and again and again, each time coming to a new understanding, a fresh realization.

The word "stuff" describes our particular bag of humanness, the hand we have been dealt. This is neither good nor bad—it is what it is, and can never be compared to anyone else's satchel of goodies. We cannot barter our liabilities. We need to accept them the same way we have embraced the parts we love.

All of us have demons we wrestle with when we go to sleep at night. These unresolved issues create a distorted lens through which we see the world. Over and over we get the opportunity to heal the dysfunctional areas and make ourselves whole. If we think we go through this once and it is resolved, we are sorely mistaken. Every time we assume that this is the end, the universe sends us another test on a more subtle level. And each time we go back and are willing to touch the vulnerability, we refine the process and get closer to the core.

At first we are overwhelmed with the enormity of the project. Our inner labor demands that we pay constant attention. We are not used to being focused, and it takes all our energy to concentrate on the work at hand. We give ourselves the microscope treatment—every word and thought is analyzed, every gesture second-guessed. At the end of the day, we are exhausted from being so vigilant.

But because we hold our resolve, we are rewarded—the intensity lessens, but the awareness remains. Rather than being painfully tied to these feelings, we deal with them as they surface, much as a skilled batter hits whatever ball is pitched. We do not judge, we just swing, knowing we can hit them all.

This is the grand game. By finally coming full circle, we experience our human condition from a completely different vantage point. It is no longer fraught with tales of woe. By simply letting it be, our humanity has become our quirky backdrop, our unique playing field.

And at day's end, it's all just stuff, no one's is any better or worse than anyone else's.

Consciousness Is A Dance— Come Dance With Me

I spent every day of ten years with my guru. From the beginning the relationship was characterized with a deep desire on my part to know what he knew. I made a vow that I would not leave India until I was sure that there was a solid place inside me, a home base I could count on. Almost to the day, ten years later, I left. I felt that core was there, and I was ready to bring what I had learned back into the world.

The years that followed were tumultuous. I had lived a monastic life and thought I might get special points for living that aesthetic lifestyle, but I quickly realized that the universe was not impressed with my spiritual quest and that I was going to have to make my way in the everyday world just like everyone else. Rather than coast, I did a lot of back peddling. Life was difficult.

It soon became abundantly clear that there were things I needed to do. I got a graduate degree and joined the working class. I also began to explore many unresolved issues from my childhood. I innately understood that life is whole, no one part any more important than any other part, and that to feel that oneness I needed to have a firm grasp on all of life, not just the parts I was good at.

The universe was not buying into a tradeoff—just because I could meditate for hours and sometimes have visions and astral travel did not mean that I could ignore my psychological and physical self. I was going to have to deal with my demons and make a meaningful life for myself.

As the years passed and the spiritual, psychological, and physical worlds merged, I began to feel complete. The process and my life had become the same, and I was no longer looking for any resolution or final resting place. Actually, the whole concept of a spiritual life was gone; it was simply a life, mine, and that was the end of it.

Then one night I had a dream, or something like a dream. I could feel myself go into another state of consciousness, and as I watched the scene unfold before me, I was in a large ballroom filled with all my friends and many people I have known throughout my life. The tables were stacked high with all kinds of delicious foods, and everyone was eating and talking, waiting for the arrival of Baba, my guru.

Soon I heard someone say, "He's coming." I could feel my heart begin to race, pounding, beating faster and faster. At one point, I thought I was going to pass out. I felt something significant was about to happen but I had no idea what it was. I heard myself saying, "You think you've done a pretty good job getting yourself together but now we'll see how together you really are." I knew that even if I had been able to fool myself all these years, I could never fool my teacher, never fool the one who had taught me.

I was standing on the other side of the room when he walked in. The crowd easily parted as he walked through the door. I trembled with fear, watching him stride with purpose across the floor. He had always been a hard taskmaster and would never rest until his disciple got the lesson; I had prepared myself for whatever was to come and steeled myself for the onslaught.

Suddenly, I realized he was walking toward me, and before I even had a chance to think about it, he was standing in front of me. There was a moment of silence as everyone stared, waiting to see what he would do.

And then it happened. My day of reckoning had come. He held his arms out in front of him, looked me right in the eye, and said, "Would you like to dance?" I remember thinking, "He's asking you to dance. He would not do that unless he wanted to dance with you. Dance with him."

I held up my arms and put my hand in his. He glided me effortlessly all around the floor, and we danced, and danced, and danced. Each fluid movement gave way to the next; I felt weightless as I moved in perfect sync with my guru. And when it was over, he thanked me for the dance.

When I woke from my "dream," I could still feel the effects of our encounter. I asked myself what had just happened and heard a voice say, without reserve, "You got it. You can dance, you can do it."

Well, maybe I can and maybe I can't. It doesn't really matter. What does matter is that I did once, and if you can do it once, you can do it again.

The dance of consciousness is a metaphor for the Divine interplay, the merging of the whole and its parts, the consummate experience of oneness. This, and nothing else, is what makes us whole.